PAST
TENSE

PAST TENSE

A MATT MOULTON MYSTERY

MICHAEL AMEDEO

First published by Level Best Books/Historia 2024

Copyright © 2024 by Michael Amedeo

First edition

ISBN: 978-1-68512-573-8

Cover art by Level Best Designs

*This book was professionally typeset on Reedsy.
Find out more at reedsy.com*

"The Past Is Never Dead. It's Not Even Past."

—WILLIAM FAULKNER

Chapter One

In the beginning, there was nothing—nothing much to worry about.

It was October 5, 1949, and it seemed like a typical day. I was hard at work, deeply plowing away at my job. In fact, my work was directly underneath me: She was a thirty-ish blonde, a brand-new client. She was as yellow as Tweety Bird and strikingly beautiful, though it was in a distant and detached kind of way: Painstakingly powder-puffed, perfumed, and pampered to carefully suppress and even hide any shade of earthiness or inconvenient humanity. I liked to be able to fully see, smell, taste, and feel my sexual partners, but you couldn't do it with this babe. She wasn't real. She was a calendar picture that took fleshly form.

So why was I sleeping with her—or at least trying to? Let me explain: I was a dick. No, I didn't work for the police, though I had struggled as a police detective for a while after I returned from the war. I was a private dick in San Francisco, working night and day all over the city. I helped needy, greedy, dirty, desperate, domineering, meddlesome, or just plain curious people solve their personal problems, specifically the kind that the police couldn't or wouldn't have anything to do with. In fact, some of these people, such as the current blonde, didn't want police or any other authorities involved at all. She paid me to find her long-lost older sister for her, but she insisted on sealing the deal in naked negotiations.

That wasn't unusual. More than a few of my female clients, including married ones, intimated that intimacy be part of the job. I've always been somewhat mystified as to the reasons why. I guess they expected a kind of cheap thrill in bedding down with a dick, who—in the movies and books—sauntered around as a kind of rebellious American hero. I admit that it also helped that I was not unpleasant to look at: I stood just under six feet tall, weighed about 170 pounds, sported wavy dark brown hair and large light blue eyes, and faced the world with no distinguishable scars or marks. Though gruff and cynical at times, I also had an inadvertently encouraging bedside manner. The clients who really knew me well sometimes called me "doc."

But I'm betting that it was partly the war that had changed my female clients and American women in general. That conflict left women to their own devices—they became independent because they had to. With their husbands and boyfriends overseas, they filled and mastered important jobs, managed their own money, handled everyday business affairs, and—most important—took responsibility for satisfying their own sexual appetites. I served in the war with a guy, an ordinarily realistic young man, who was delirious with pride upon learning in a letter that his dear wife was pregnant. But as I saw it, there was a problem here: He hadn't been back home for many months, and so it really couldn't have been his child in her womb. That fact apparently didn't occur to him, and I certainly wasn't going to be the one to deflate his dream. His wife took her sexuality into her own hands, and now the poor sap couldn't see that those hands were dirty.

Of course, women clients weren't holding a gun to my head: I didn't have to succumb to their carnal suggestions. I had my own women, and I had gone under covers with more than a few of them. But sleeping with a client was good for business, and that was why I did it any chance I got, her looks or manner be damned. Sex often meant a greater payday. And more important, it made clients more cooperative. They came to me wearing a mask, hiding a lot of facts and reluctant to tell me even those secrets I needed to know to do their job. The promise of sex encouraged them to lower the veil as they dropped the panties—or at least most of the time it did.

And that brings me back to the client in question, the prone Amy Barrett from, as she put it, "out East." After fifteen minutes of passivity, she was starting to show signs of life, finally emitting a kind of muffled scream that seemed to say, "Excuse me for letting that out." It was essentially a drawn-out fart of a climax. The further surprise was that I also let go, though it came—so to speak—with more authority and enthusiasm.

"Matt Moulton, you are a wonderful lover. I don't know if I've ever felt more satisfied," she said as she turned her back on me to lie on her side. She was killing me with affection.

"Miss Barrett, you were pretty good yourself," I lied. "You talk as if you've had a lot of experience."

"Well, I'm a beautiful woman, aren't I?" she asked, with a genteel sassiness.

"You are that, Miss Barrett. Yes, you are." Moving up right behind her and embracing her around the waist, I then returned to the more important business at hand. "You said you last saw your older sister Dorothy back in 1942, just before she went across the country to San Francisco. Now tell me again why you waited so long to search for her."

She sighed in the same way you do when a precocious little kid asks too many inconvenient questions. "Well, as I said, I was writing to her regularly in 'Frisco until, after about a year, the letters started coming back as 'return to sender.' That scared me. But I did nothing about it because the war was on, and I was so worried about my boyfriend overseas. We broke up when he returned home, but then I became tied up in a couple of other serious relationships. Suddenly, I realized it was almost 1950, and I still didn't know where poor Sis was. Time just got away from me, you know. I don't know where it went."

"Yes, though sometimes time can lag and linger," I said in a sad, thoughtful, mildly contrarian tone. She ignored me because my feelings had nothing to do with her.

Her story itself seemed to have changed a little, and I didn't know how much of it I believed. It wasn't any one individual fact that bothered me; it was the implied motivation for her search that left me wondering. I didn't exactly buy the sweet and worried sister routine. But I let her peddle it without a challenge.

"Does your sister have the same last name?"

"Oh, ah, no. Her last name is Worthington," she said. It took her a brief eternity to get that name out. "She was married for a year and, ah, kept the name."

"In that photo you gave me, she looks a lot like you. The big turquoise eyes are the same. But she's just a little less blonde and a little more down-to-earth," I ventured to say.

She quickly became offended. "What's that supposed to mean?" My remark violated her vanity.

I then rallied. "I only mean that you're a lot more Hollywood than she is. But hey, you're both gorgeous." I tried to change the subject. "By the way, what was her former husband's first

4

name? Might he be living here, too?"

She paused, as if her mind momentarily froze, and said: "It's, ah, Harry and I think he still lives out East."

"And where is that, Miss Barrett?"

"You know, out East."

In her case, sex wasn't the informational aphrodisiac that I had hoped it would be. "Is Barrett your maiden name?"

"Well, ah, oh, yes." With her face hidden, I couldn't see the look of the lie.

"Could she be using that name instead of Worthington?"

"Well, ah, no. She would use Worthington."

"Oh, okay. Well, I'll start my search with her last known San Francisco address and then see where that leads. Where can I reach you?"

She raised herself halfway up to reach for her purse on the table, placing her bare behind directly in front of my face. I didn't mind; it would have made a great calendar shot for bringing heat to a chillier month—say, January. "I'll call you for updates," she insisted. "Meanwhile, let me give you some more money." She handed me five more hundred-dollar bills—the sex accomplished something.

I gave her a toothy grin. "Thank you, Miss Barrett. My bank account sends you its best wishes. Now, would you like a drink, say a bourbon or scotch?"

"Oh yes, bourbon and water would be nice! May I use your powder room?" she coyly asked with a forced smile.

"Sure, as long as you stop calling it that. I stopped using powder as a base ages ago," I said in an affected tone.

As soon as she took her clothes into the bathroom, I darted for her purse on the living room table, looking for some real facts. I found a pretentiously pearled wallet stuffed with fifties and hundreds—this doll was loaded. But I needed to locate an ID, and that almost didn't happen because a shrill noise made me jump and all but drop everything.

It sounded like: "Matt, where's my drink?" Though not an unusual question, it came out of nowhere and hit me like the most piercing fire alarm.

"Coming right up, Miss Barrett." I mixed a strong one on my well-stocked bar cart and took it to her. "Dearie, I have your fire water." She answered the door in the altogether and seductively reached for the glass. I could only marvel that if she enjoyed sex as much as she promoted it, this client would be a real babe of a bedmate.

Returning to the purse search, I finally located a driver's license; it was from Pennsylvania with a Philadelphia address. It turned out that she really was an Amy, but that her last name was Worthington, her sister's supposed married handle. I also found a business card from the San Francisco Hilton, a chichi place downtown. You didn't have to be rich to stay there, but it certainly helped. I was glad I sacked her purse: Those things could provide a personal lowdown in a hurry.

Reemerging from the bathroom in her almost too-perfect form, Miss Barrett gulped down the rest of her glass, gasped, coughed a little, and then said, "You mixed a pretty stiff drink. Are you trying to get me drunk?"

I played along with her. "Sure. How else am I going to get you back into bed? Maybe we can get the mattress springs squeaking again."

"Matt, all you have to do is ask," she insisted as she hiccuped.

"I love to ask things. For example, why did your sister leave the East for San Francisco?" That broke the spell of suggestiveness. She didn't become curt, but she came close when she impatiently answered, "Who knows? Dorothy always went her own way, and Dad loved her for it.

"But Matt, I've got to go now." She picked up her purse, flashed a quick beam my way, and then mustered the passion to peck me on the lips. When it came to sex, she was even more of a businessperson than I was.

"Bye-bye, I'll be in touch," she said as she slipped into the living room and out my door.

"Wait, take my card."

"Thanks, Matt. Ta-ta!" She puckered her puffy lips, airmailing me another kiss.

Pondering the potential relations between Amy and her sister, I lit a cigarette, poured another drink, and called Sara Manson, my secretary and office partner.

"Hi Sara, it's Matt. How are things?"

"Oh, hi, Matt," she said in her throaty voice. It typically seemed to get gently deeper as the long day wore on. "It's been slow around here. Just some phone calls and a little research. On the crazy side, Joe Greene came in with his last payment, and he looked petrified and pale, as if death were tagging along!"

"Well, he should be," I said. "He was three weeks late with my money, and his job was an expensive one. I told him that I was going to break his arm if he didn't pay up today." I had done several jobs for Greene, a fat and blustery small businessman with a bad wig. When my work brought good news, he paid quickly. But when he didn't like what I found, he dawdled on his payment plan. That's what happened here: He hired me to spy on his wife, and I discovered that she was sleeping with the enemy—his more successful brother, Tom. I had the photos to prove it. He didn't like the truth of brotherly love.

"Oh, Matt, why do you have to threaten violence? You're a

much better person than that."

"Well, you're biased," I said, in a voice that tried to sound irritated. "Besides, you know I sometimes have to act as my own collection agency. The threat of broken bones and bloodied lips helps us pay the bills.

"But Sara, I didn't call to talk about pounding deadbeats. I need you to do an emergency research job for me. Do you remember Amy Barrett?"

"Oh yeah, that va-va-voom babe who came in this morning?"

"Yes. Her last name is actually Worthington, and she lives in Philadelphia, Pennsylvania. Her lost sister is Dorothy, who came out here seven years ago. Could

you spend a couple days digging up information on them? Amy is thirty-one, and her sister is two or three years older."

"Sure thing, Matt! Anything else you need?

"No, dearie, that's it. Go back to sleep. G'night!"

I would begin searching for the missing Dorothy tomorrow. Little did I know I would never see her sister Amy again.

Chapter Two

In a sense, houses and apartment buildings are people, too. They live, they thrive or struggle, and they ultimately die. They get their lifeblood from the succession of human beings who live in them.

The sprawling, middle-aged, three-story brick building at 2012 Cascade Drive—Dorothy Worthington's last known residence—looked as if it had been living a hard life. It wasn't part of a slum; the surrounding neighborhood, though in decline, was still more or less neatly working-class. But this building seemed to exhale a more desperate air, suggesting that it was one of the last places struggling people could go to avoid the void of complete squalor.

Perhaps the current season made it look worse than it really was. San Francisco was generally a soft blur kind of place because of its wateriness (bordering on both a bay and an ocean) and its romantically cool and foggy clime. But fall tended to be the town's summer, and this day's weather reflected that with both blaring sunshine and the stark steam heat of ninety degrees. The combination made everything seem sharper and harder. It exposed and accented the building's sagging wrinkles and overall physical breakdown: its cracked and eroded base; its disheveled lawn, flecked with the occasional piece of garbage or fly-covered dog dropping; its smudged windows, broken blinds, and torn shades; and its one newer addition, a windowless, heavyweight, prison-like front door, which didn't close all the way. No, somehow, it just didn't seem like the kind of place that someone like Amy's sister would call home.

I rang the first doorbell I saw; it belonged to a Theodore H. Slugg. He rang back, and the first door on the first floor opened with a powerful emission of stale beer and unwashed male body odor. A weary-eyed Mr. Slugg, a short and balding man with protruding cheeks and an ill-fitting t-shirt, demanded to know my business. He spoke from a living room that was like a tossed and wilted salad of this and that, here and there. His right paw clutched a racing form like a blackjack.

"Hello, my name is Matt Moulton. I'm sorry to bother you, Mac, but I need some information."

"Who wants ta know what?" uttered Slugg. "Are you from the police?" He coughed hard into his rolled-up racing form. I thought I was going to need to pound on his back.

"Oh no, I'm a private investigator looking for a missing person."

"Well, good, 'cause I'm tired of cops comin' around botherin' me about my brother. He went ahead and served his time in the pen for armed robbery, and now any

fuckin' time there's a hold-up in this city, they come by askin' me questions. I mean, why the Hell me?" Slugg went on, getting louder: "I tell them, he doesn't live here no more! And I donna where he is.'"

"I'm sorry to hear about your problem. But again, I'm not a cop. Have you lived in this building for long?"

He calmed down. "Bout ten years." It sounded as if he were referring to a prison term.

"Do you remember a resident by the name of Dorothy Worthington?"

"Worthington?" Slugg's eyes rolled slowly around as if he were literally scanning his memory.

"Nah, the name doesn't ring a bell," he claimed.

"She lived here about seven years ago, and this is what she looked like around that time." I handed him Dorothy's picture.

He brightened and even hinted at a smile. "Oh yeah, yeah, yeah, I remember her now. She was the pretty lady who lived with the Slotkowski family. I used to like to watch her walk— she was a real looker, with a nice round behind."

"Good, you knew her behind. But did you know her at all?'

"Know her? Naw, not really. We never talked, except maybe to say 'how ya doin.'"

"Do the Slotkowskis still live here?"

"Yep, they still stay in one of the bigger apartments upstairs, 3D." He seemed proud to know that.

"Thanks for the info, pal." I turned to leave.

"Yeah, I gotta get goin', too. I tend bar at the Longshore Inn on Touhy. It's a great hangout. Kinda homey, ya know? Ever been there?"

"No, I haven't." I stopped and pulled a few singles from my wallet. "But why don't you have a few drinks on me?"

I was surprised he could move so fast. He grabbed the money, quickly counted it, and thanked me. I guess I made his day.

I went up to 3D, and just as I was about to knock, the door opened. A startled woman stood there facing me. She had carefully brushed graying hair and what you would call a once handsome face, the visage of a strong, perhaps domineering woman in a losing battle with time, tragedy, and disappointment. You had the feeling that she was once a carefree tomboy.

Her light hazel eyes had the watery, high-wattage look of someone who had been drinking for hours. My guess was confirmed when she opened her mouth and let out a bouquet of wine—1949 vintage.

"Ooh, I beg your pardon. Are you looking for someone?" said the woman.

"I'm looking for the Slotkowski residence."

"You found it. I'm Mrs. Slotkowski," she said in a steely but helpful manner.

"Pleased to meet you. I'm Matt Moulton, a private investigator. I'm looking for information about someone who apparently used to live with you—Dorothy Worthington."

"Worthington? Oh yes, Dorothy. Ah, won't you come in?"

I walked into a clean, precisely arranged, modestly maintained apartment that looked as if it were frozen in time. It was mothball city: Everything seemed preserved from ten years ago or more. I almost expected to see a calendar hanging somewhere turned to a page in the distant past. It looked exactly the same when Dorothy had stayed there.

"Please have a seat, Mr. Moulton. I'd offer you a drink, except I've run out of alcohol. There's not a drop in the house. I was going out to buy a couple of bottles when you arrived. Would you like me to make coffee?"

"No thank you, Mrs. Slotkowski. Coffee's a lot like life—it either keeps me awake or gives me nightmares. I can't win with java. I'm fine." Besides, I gathered that she didn't want coffee. She kept tasting something in her mouth, although there didn't seem to be anything there. Her slight tipsiness and that intense alcoholic stare told me that she wanted a real drink. But she appeared to be a veteran drinker who had learned how to control herself and restrain her habit when necessary. I felt

12

as if we were going to have a productive talk.

"Mrs. Slotkowski...."

"Please call me Rita."

"And you may call me Matt. Rita, what can tell me about Dorothy and her stay with you?"

"That gal was a real sweetheart," she said, her voice softening. "Let's see...Dorothy first came into our lives when she responded to our room-for-rent ad sometime back in early '42. We were a little wary about letting a stranger stay in our home, but she immediately touched our hearts and put our minds at ease. She was very gentle and considerate. I remember she kept talking about how her living here would be a help to us. She kept mentioning us! It was as if she were applying for a job to take care of Charlie and me. Imagine that? What a darling." She lost herself in the memory.

"I'm sorry, Rita, who's Charlie?"

"Oh, Charlie's my son. He was a boy when Dorothy moved in. Now he's a man: Charlie signed up for the Navy last year and plans to make a career of it," she said with a kind of forced bravado. "Picture that—Dorothy sometimes babysat him, and now he's a man serving his country! But anyway, his going away left me all alone, a woman without a family. You see, I have nobody because I also lost my husband, Robert. He died of cancer when Charlie was small," she almost whispered through a sob. Her eyes watered further even as the artificial, alcohol-induced light in them began to dim.

"My heart goes out to you, Rita. Loneliness is a cruel acquaintance," I said, having spent many hours with it myself. I let a few long seconds pass and then asked, "Did Dorothy hold down a job while she was here?"

She rubbed her eyes but failed to wipe away the misery of

a frozen time and lonely place. "Oh, yes, as the night shift manager at the In and Out Grill, I was able to pull strings and get her hired as a carhop on days. She fit in very well there. But she didn't seem to spend a lot of the money she earned. She was very thrifty. She told me that she dreamed of accumulating enough resources to start her own little business. That seemed to be her driving ambition."

"Did she say what kind of business?"

"No, not exactly. She said she had earned a college degree and become interested in international matters. But she didn't say too much more about her plans than that. Dorothy just sounded smart about anything she ever talked about." Rita seemed to become more clearly sober and more focused the more she talked.

"Did she make friends at work?

"I heard she had good relations with everyone. The problem was that the jobs at In and Out Grill were literally in-and-out jobs. People stayed a few months and then left.

So I think it would be tough to find anybody who had really gotten to know her. Dorothy herself was there only about eight months or so. I've been a part of the place for years, but of course, I'm old and have few other options."

"Yes, I know what you mean. I've seen and heard a lot of sad stories. The Land of Opportunity doesn't always offer many second chances. Oftentimes, you have to stick with what you've got." I was no false flag waver. I knew all about the red, white, and blue, but there was way too much of the last color for my taste.

"Do you know whether Dorothy formed any close friendships or dated anyone?"

"I know for certain that she dated an important-looking older

14

man—I saw him a few times from the window on my days off. He always wore a conservative suit and tie and picked her up in this large blue car, which looked to be something from the late 30s—about as new as you could get in those war years. He would toot the horn when he arrived. She never invited him into the house because I think she assumed that it would impose on us."

"Did she ever talk about an ex-husband?" I asked.

"No, she told me she never married."

"Hmm. What happened when she left here for good? Did she quit her job at the same time?"

"Everything happened in a rush. One day, Dorothy sat us down and announced that she was quitting her job and moving out at the end of the week. Charlie cried—and I cried inside, too. It felt like we were losing a member of the family. She was very reassuring about it, insisting that she would stay in touch with us. She left the impression that she would be living nearby, in the San Francisco area. But we never heard from her again," she said, her voice trailing off. Life had let Rita down once more—or so her now sorry eyes seemed to say.

"Aside from stuff about college, did she ever share any information with you about her life before 'Frisco?"

"I knew she had a younger sister and brother, and she sometimes told stories about their experiences growing up on the East Coast and how different it was back there. But the details were always fuzzy. I never even learned what city she came from—and I felt funny about asking. Dorothy was outgoing about everything but her personal life. I wish I had been able to get closer to her," she said, her hands reaching out to the big bygone.

"Yes, Rita, I wish you had learned more about Dorothy, too—

it would have made my job easier. But in the end, we're all kind of a mystery, aren't we? It's hard to find out much about anyone."

I'm not sure my comments went over well. She looked at me with a confused expression that seemed to ask, "Then what do we have private detectives for?" I sometimes wondered the same thing.

I had tortured this poor woman long enough—she needed some refreshment. "Rita, I'm done, but would you permit me to buy you a drink? I promise to stop giving

you the third degree about Dorothy and the past." Her eyes celebrated, and I'm sure her tongue did a dance, too. "Oh, thank you, Matt, that sounds wonderful."

After finishing with Rita, I pursued leads on a couple of smaller jobs. But in the back of my mind, I kept thinking about the Philadelphia sisters and where that case might go. I needed help and hoped that Sara would provide it in the office tomorrow.

Chapter Three

I worked in the middle of nowhere. Though it was just about a mile from downtown, my office was in a five-story building in a neighborhood that could best be called darkly dissonant. Sure, it had its lively spots—a lot of cheap office buildings, several decent bars, a few okay grub joints, and a big old movie theater. But to get to those places, you had to navigate through a well-populated Skid Row, down a few eerily deserted streets, or past sometimes sleazy and even sinister characters lurking on the sidewalks. I heard that at one time, just after World War I, it was a bustling neighborhood. But the Great Depression in the 30s brought it to its knees, and ten years later, it still wasn't able to get back up.

The jewel of the neighborhood was the Palace movie theater, and it sat right next door to my building. The large neon letters of its vertically arranged marquee individually flashed on and flashed off in a decidedly hypnotic way outside my window, and on some darker nights, that repetition drove me crazy. I would sometimes close the blinds, but it didn't entirely black out the mocking light. Maybe it was better not to have a neighborhood jewel.

But now, it was a new day. I parked my gray 1941 Dodge Sedan in front of that very theater and went up to my unadorned, two-room, fifth-floor office. I was looking forward to seeing Sara.

But first, let me provide a little biography. Sara was a tall, big-boned, 40-year-old bottle blonde with a bit of a problem: She was living the wrong life. She had two kids, and she dearly loved them, devoting herself to being the best mother she could be. But in a different world, Sara probably should have been doing something else—something more daring and adventurous. Whenever I would tell her about one of the many perilous scrapes I got myself into on this job, she would initially turn motherly and almost scold me for taking chances. But as I related more details about it, a sense of wonder and enchantment would often come into her rapt, dark brown eyes. It was as if she was living through me, imagining herself fighting off that danger. She wanted to know more. After a couple of such stories, she even asked me to take her out and teach her how to handle a gun. I obliged, thinking—and maybe hoping— that her new knowledge would help get me out of a tight corner one day.

Sara showed a detective's instincts, but she had to settle for playing them out on the phone, behind a desk, or in the library. She'd do research and gather info that always made me a wiser, more effective dick. And if I was the one who usually had a feel for who not to trust, she always seemed to know who was worthwhile, who you could take a chance on. But, whatever the type, she was usually a great judge of people. That's why, in the end, she was my "dicktress," an irreplaceable, indispensable junior partner.

Sara's insight into people failed her at least once, however. In 1929, when she was in college, she met a charmingly complicated student named George Manson and fell hard for him. When the economy crashed a little while later, it foiled their college dreams

, and the couple reached for what they saw as the next best thing—marriage. Twelve years and two children later, Uncle Sam called, and George reluctantly answered. Perhaps he foresaw what fate had in store for him next: stepping on a stray grenade during battle on a Pacific Island. It partially malfunctioned, and that fact saved his life. But he still lost his right leg and—it seemed—his courage and determination as well. He just didn't know how to handle misfortune. When he returned home, he stayed there, spending most of his time feeling sorry for himself. Sara had to become the family breadwinner, and that benefited me when I opened my gumshoe business in 1947.

I was thinking about all that when I entered the two-room office, but Sara immediately brought up what was on the back of my mind.

"Afternoon, Matt. I have a lot to tell you about the Worthington case," she said from the curvy confines of an aquamarine business jacket and skirt. It looked a little wrinkled, and her long, razor-cut hair looked a little tousled, and both were signs that she'd been hard at work all morning. "You better sit down. You're not going to believe what I've found."

"Okay, doll." I removed my light gray jacket and black hat, grabbed a chair, and pushed it closer to Sara's desk. And she was right. I wasn't easily shocked—and then there was this.

"Your client and her missing sister and a younger brother are part of the Rufus Worthington family, whose mining and manufacturing fortune is now worth $200 million and counting. And that's a low-end estimate." Her wide-eyed, open-mouthed look dared me to believe it.

At first, that figure just didn't figure. I got up to pour a drink, gulped it down, and asked the fateful question, "Why would a family that rich be coming to me for help? What the Hell could I do for them?"

"Rufus is eighty years old and dying. The only one of his kids that he has any use for is Dorothy," said Sara. "The general dope is that he's leaving her all or most of his money. So naturally, he's undertaken an expensive nationwide search to find her. What your client Amy, his younger daughter, is doing appears to be a separate thing."

Sara's research supported my suspicions about Amy and her chilly, manipulative, businesslike nature. "Amy started her own underground search using something that her father maybe didn't have—Dorothy's last known address. Since it was in San Francisco, she hired a Frisco dick such as me to do the hunting. If I got lucky and found Dorothy, Amy could make a direct pitch to her for a share of the fortune. It makes sense," I realized. "Her sister's welfare is secondary. Amy's all about the money, and a wealthy husband doesn't seem to be in the offing."

"Are you closing in on where sis might be?" said Sara, being painfully direct.

"No, but I think I may know why she left home. I get the impression that she didn't appreciate the easy money that came with being a Worthington. She wanted to make her own way, start her own business, live her own life. She was an independent and ambitious person, and perhaps that was at least part of the reason she was daddy's little favorite."

Then Sara further complicated things. "We keep talking about Dorothy and Amy, but what about brother Peter?

"Well, what did you find out about him?"

"He's the youngest of the children and the family's black sheep—a spoiled and nasty brat. He's been lazy and irresponsible, prone to creating embarrassing scandals involving alcohol and the police. When he was nineteen, he got charged with involuntary manslaughter, but thanks to Daddy's high-priced attorneys, he beat the rap. The trial was all over the Philly papers for months."

"Whoa. It sounds as if Peter needs the big money even more than Amy does. He wouldn't be able to live free without it. Has he turned up here in your research?" I asked.

"I have seen no trace of him in the Bay Area so far."

"Don't be surprised if he turns up soon. His future may depend on getting to Dorothy first," I said. "Green colors everything in this one."

I poured another drink. "Anything else?"

"That's the gist of the story," she said.

"Thanks for everything, angel. I'm going back in my office to mull things over."

"Let me know if I can help," she said.

Behind my closed door, I had the privacy to openly worry, to maybe even allow it to show on my face. It's one of the advantages of being alone. In wondering where Dorothy disappeared, I thought back to her plans to open a business. Is that where I would find her? Where might that be?

I pulled out the San Francisco Yellow Pages and flipped around to several categories touching on international business. I spent a little time in the tourism section, but none of the business names suggested Dorothy, assuming she hadn't named it something like A-1 Tourism or Atlas Travel.

I also read through the many listings for international trade companies, but nothing caught my eye until the very last one: Worth Import/Export. Worth? Could Dorothy be associated with that one? I took down the address and phone number.

But before I could make a call, my door swung open, and Lieutenant Gilbert Brannigan and three of his thug detectives stormed in. He was talking angry, fast, and loud, and I couldn't make out one word of it. He looked and sounded like a Gestapo agent shouting in German, an image that perfectly captured this slick-haired, oily-skinned horror of a man, my former boss in the San Francisco Detective Bureau. We enforced two kinds of law there: city law and Brannigan's law, with the latter always coming first. He ran things as an arrogant, arbitrary, egotistical tyrant, and, of course, he hated me because I thought for myself and didn't like taking orders.

As he continued to lean over my desk and rant, heaving his toilet breath into my face, Sara buzzed me on the intercom. I clicked to hear her say: "I'm sorry, Matt. There was no stopping him."

But I had to at least try to slow him down. I stood up, readying for battle but hoping for peace. "Now lieutenant, calm down. What's your business here, and why do you need so much muscle to carry it out? I'm just one guy who runs a business."

Though he was still boiling, he turned down the flame a little bit. "Moulton, one of your 'business' clients, told us that you're terrorizing him with threats."

Uh, oh, the deadbeat Greene double-crossed me, and that made me mad. "Terrorizing? No, I didn't threaten a hair on the head of any client. You got the wrong dope, lieutenant. I haven't broken any laws, and you don't have the right to come charging in here harassing my secretary and brutalizing me with your bullshit."

22

I had forgotten about Brannigan's law. Out of nowhere, a huge fist crashed into my face with a painful reminder. The force knocked me down into my wheeled chair, which crashed into the inside window ledge and almost into the blinds and through the window.

The punch struck my nose and cheek but went to my head: For what seemed like forever, I could hear little and see even less. I picked up the words, "Moulton, you've always been a troublemaking asswipe, and you'll never change," but I didn't know from where and to whom they came.

As the brain haze started to dissipate, I staggered to my feet. I could barely open my mouth and move my lips, but I managed to utter, "Lieutenant, you're a brave man when you're hiding behind a badge and a trio of thugs. Now either arrest me or get the fuck out of here." I thought: "No problem, Matt, antagonize him again. He has only four inches and fifty pounds on you. And when he gets tired, he can sic his rabid backup muscle on you."

A hint of rage returned to the lieutenant's eyes. "Moulton, I'll have your license pulled!"

"Okay, Lieutenant. I'll go to the DA and tell him all about you. Then we'll be even. Fair enough?" I said, with a cutting smile that tried to draw blood.

He hated to lose. But he also recognized that, for now, continuing to taunt and squeeze me wasn't in his best interests. The lieutenant shook his head, signaled to his men, and led them out the door.

I felt like a defeated victor. I prevailed in the standoff, but now I had to find a way to tend to the wounds to my nose and to my pride. Sara could help with the nose. Drawing a bead on Dorothy would help with the pride.

Chapter Four

Answers never came easy. And that was certainly proving true with the intriguing lead of Worth Import/Export, where no one was even picking up the phone.

So I headed to its office in the Woodward Building, an ornate, exotic twenty-one-story mystery in the center of San Francisco's downtown. It was difficult to size up this place visually because it seemed to be three buildings melded into one, two of them side-by-side and a third—softly rounded—sprouting out of the top of the other two. Whenever I saw it, I wondered what I was looking at and what it was hiding.

I found Worth Import/Export on its eighteenth floor, but the door was locked in the middle of business hours. Was the staff taking a late and lengthy lunch? I didn't expect to find out anything in Philbin Accounting, the larger office next door, but I walked in there anyway. I caught the receptionist at a busy time: She was alternately and awkwardly typing and filing—filing her nails, that is. Hiding behind too much makeup, the doll appeared to be someone in her late teens pretending to be an adult. Her chewing and snapping of gum undermined that pose.

"Excuse me, Sister, do you know anything about Worth

Import/Export, the business next door?"

"Oh gosh, the police found a dead body there a few days ago," she said breathlessly in a high-pitched voice. "It's been closed ever since."

Uh, oh. "Did they say who died?"

"I don't know the details. Let me go get Mr. Philbin."

Mr. Philbin was a long man with somber eyes and an endless chin on a pale-white face. "May I help you, sir?" he drawled. Though he apparently was a numbers man, his funereal look and manner suggested that he knew a lot about death. Maybe he counted dead bodies.

"Do you know about what happened next door?"

"Oh goodness, Miss Martin was murdered. The police said she was shot in the chest. It…"

I interrupted him with my main concerns. "Did you actually witness anything?"

"No, I just heard about the shooting."

"Who was Miss Martin?"

"She was Barbara Martin, the owner of Worth. And she was the nicest person you'd ever want to meet. I just can't imagine why anyone would want to kill her. It's very sad…"

"How old was she? Can you describe her?"

"I guess she was about thirty-five, thirty-six. But she looked younger. Very pretty—big blue eyes, dark brown hair. It's a tragedy."

"Dark hair?"

"Yes, very dark hair and very light skin."

"Was she a California native?

"She was an American, but I don't know if she was from here or from elsewhere in the country."

"Did anyone else work in her office?

"No, it was just Miss Martin, and that surprised me. She needed help. The company was doing brisk business due to the country's increased trade with Europe and Asia. I guess she had to work long hours to get everything done." Philbin seemed to be intimate with the idea of long working hours without help.

"Well, I'm very sorry, Mr. Philbin, thank you. She doesn't appear to be the person I was looking for. Good day."

But I wasn't kidding myself: Deep down, I knew that Barbara Martin could have been Dorothy Worthington. They were the same age, they seemed to have the same general personality, and they were both internationally inclined.

I became more alarmed after I visited the city's Office of Small Business. I learned that Worth Import/Export had received its business license in March 1943, which would have been about the time Dorothy moved out of the Slotkowski apartment.

I needed to find out more about Martin, to at least see her face in a picture. Sara looked around for me and discovered that Martin's death had largely been uncovered in the papers, except for a small notice in the Chronicle. A murder in the middle of downtown got only one hundred and fifty words and no picture in the main city newspaper? That was strange and more than a little suspicious.

I had to turn to the Detective Bureau for help, and that could only come through Gina Harner. She was the bureau's administrative assistant, but that title trivialized her role. Everything that went in and went out of the department passed through her. While she didn't manage anyone or investigate anything, she kept track of where the detectives were sent and where the case files were stored—in other words, she knew where all the bodies were buried. Having unlimited knowledge and access, she held quiet power—and she handled it smartly.

Still, I was initially wary of turning to her because of our past together: She was my girlfriend while I was at the bureau and for a short time thereafter. Though colleagues should probably never date each other, I just couldn't resist her. She was like the morning time in human form. Gina had a fresh face, bright light brown eyes, and full, saucy lips, and she radiated a kind of raw and warming energy. It so animated her long legs and twisty hips that she seemed to be dancing as she walked. It was all so natural. I guess I loved Gina.

The problem was that we didn't see eye-to-eye on the reason for our eventual break-up. I insisted that it was because I was incapable of devoting myself to one woman, even if I loved her. And, frankly, love itself was a foreign influence on me, some import from an imaginary land far, far away. My explanation crushed her, but she also hinted that it was hiding something more real—her race. You see, Gina was a Negro.

Her beauty wasn't dark, and it wasn't light either, though her color—or race—didn't matter to me, or at least I didn't think it did. But it sure mattered to others. As we went about the city together, we turned heads, with a few too many of the faces showing disapproval and even contempt. We even got a similar, if more subtle, reaction from black people. The world was essentially wagging its finger at us, railing away that a Negro woman romantically paired with a white man was freakish and maybe illicit.

If the outside world's reaction was bad, the bureau's was worse, especially from a guy like Brannigan. That wasn't a surprise. The lieutenant scorned Negroes, rarely taking their reports about crime seriously. And while he brutalized many kinds of suspects, he seemed to save the worst treatment for black ones. The great leader booted around the whites and

Asians, but he ground his heel into the blacks.

Despite all that, Brannigan became obsessed with Gina. He was always leering at her, always speculating and joking with his dick pals about the state of her love life. It appeared that she was this racist cop's darkest, most forbidden fantasy. And perhaps I undermined that fantasy when I started dating her. I immediately went from being someone he disliked to someone he abhorred. My long-term career prospects in the bureau plummeted, which would have been terrible only if I had liked working at that crazy place. Seeing Gina every day would have been the only good thing about staying there.

It became increasingly obvious to me that the Worthington case was not the only reason I wanted and needed to see her. I surprised her with a phone call and arranged a dinner date for that night at our favorite place, the Tenderloin, a restaurant and nightclub at the top of one of San Francisco's hilly streets.

Although it was a large and open place consisting of a bandstand, a dance floor, a long bar, and a main room of six dozen or so tables and rounded booths, the Tenderloin conveyed a real sense of intimacy, helped—no doubt—by its subdued lighting and low ceiling. People left you alone there. Hell, management left you alone there, despite being controlled by organized crime.

Its food was relatively good, but it often tasted even better because it was set to some of the best, some of the most romantic, jazzed-up live swing music you could find in San Francisco. When the head waiter showed us to our booth, the band's slim black female vocalist—backed by a piano, a deep-throated bass, a saxophone, and a couple of improvisational horns—was crooning "Too Marvelous for Words."

I smiled to myself and agreed with the song: Gina looked

too marvelous for words this night. She wore—and gave life to—a sleek, low-cut, beige evening dress whose spaghetti straps seemed ready to slip off her shoulders altogether. I would have been okay with that. Oh, in honor of her, I even wore my brand-new light blue bow tie.

Putting dinner off for later, we ordered mixed drinks, and I lit her cigarette.

"So Matt, to what do I owe the honor of your asking me out tonight," she asked, with a smile that seemed to have suspicions.

"It's been too long since we last saw each other, doll. I've really missed you," I said, mustering up the courage to be truthful.

She had the most expressive eyes of any woman I had ever met. Without moving any other part of her face, she could embrace you with them, reject you with them, and do just about any variation in between. In this instance, her eyes quickly went from a warm embrace to a sweet chide—and the words supported her. "I've missed you, too, Matt. But why don't you try using your phone more often? It would give us the chance to talk between sightings."

"Very funny. But you know how it is: It's the dick work— it's got me running around day and night. And as to getting on the phone more, that would just encourage me to talk too much and say something more to hurt you. I don't want to keep making excuses about the break-up."

"Yes, Matt, the break-up still hurts. But I'm learning how powerless we all are. I'm not going to change you, you're not going to change me, and we're certainly not going to change the world. So what's the sense of grieving over everything that goes wrong?"

I was a little jealous of how well she seemed to be adjusting. "Well, please don't give up on me that easily," I said in a voice that tried to hide my begging tone.

Her eyes shined and then quickly shaded. "Ha! Now I got you where I want you," she said in a mock fiendish manner. "But seriously, I'll never completely give up on you. I've just become more realistic about the strange world we live in."

"Well, sweetheart, it's about time—you've only been surrounded by thieves, con artists, rapists, and murderers for four years. That should be enough to make anyone realistic."

She smiled and took my hand, and we ordered dinner as the band babe delivered some wonderfully bittersweet renditions.

We ate brook trout and wild rice and reminisced about our times together. Then, it became time for less personal business. "Gina, as I hinted on the phone, I have a personal favor to ask of you. It's about one of my cases."

"Uh, oh. Well, okay: Ask away, Matt." Her wide eyes seemed to be listening.

"The authorities hushed up the downtown murder of a young businesswoman last week. Her name was Barbara Martin, and she generally fits the profile of a differently named rich doll I've been searching for. Are they one and the same? I can't tell without seeing a picture of Martin and maybe getting a gander at the file—or the general information—the bureau has on her. Can you help me?"

"Wow, I remember a little about that case—what a sorry mess it was! I got the sense it was politically sensitive, but I couldn't tell exactly why. Sure, Matt, I'll try to get your stuff. But I'm taking a big risk, especially in this situation. I'll have to go about it in a careful way. It might take some time." She tapped her spoon on the table in the rhythm of a ticking clock.

"Yeah, sure. Thank you, dear. But don't take any unnecessary chances. I can't afford to support any unemployed lovers, no matter how smart and gorgeous they are."

Her eyes were amused. "Matt Moulton, you're all heart."

I didn't want to take her home yet, and so we drove up and down the streets and through the thick fog. The environment seemed to both promise romance and threaten danger, and I wasn't in the mood for either one of them.

I finally parked the car and walked her to her apartment building's door. "Come on up and stay for a while, Matt."

The invitation felt like Christmas. But that meant I couldn't just take, I had to give, too—and that wasn't in the cards tonight. I wasn't in the mood to make love to a loved one. "No, sweetheart, I have things to do." I put my hands on her waist and bent down with a long but close-mouthed kiss. She responded by wrapping her arms around me and opening her mouth to my kiss. The start of a pounding passion returned. I was a split-second away from completely succumbing to her. But I suddenly pulled away. "Good night, dear. Let me know when you have something for me."

She looked confused and abandoned. I had hurt Gina again.

Chapter Five

It was a long night, and it wasn't going to end anytime soon. Both Sara and I were still in the office, tending to unfinished business. I was reading over a blackmail letter that one of my married clients had just received from an ex-girlfriend. Did we need to take it seriously? What evidence could the babe produce? Suddenly, Sara rang me on the intercom.

"Matt, a gentleman would like to see you. Are you up for a potential client tonight?"

"Sure, Sara, send him in."

I was still studying the letter when I sensed something looming over me. I looked up and saw the potential client—a tall guy in a brown hat and beige trench coat with the collar turned up. His eyes were staring, and his face was flashing, the latter a reflection of the theater's marquee next door. How in the Hell did he open the door and enter the room without making a sound? For a split second, I couldn't even tell if he was breathing.

"Mr. Moulton, may I sit down?"

His soft, deep voice roused me out of my trance. "Oh, I'm sorry, take a seat."

He removed his hat, sat down, and drew closer to me,

revealing blonde-haired, high cheek-boned, granite-jawed good looks. My best guess was that he had been around for somewhere close to forty years, but—oddly enough—all that time hadn't added any character to his face. He seemed authoritatively anonymous, like a well-designed, department-store mannequin in the business wear department. He had a face that was easy to forget if you saw it only once.

"I need your help looking for someone," said the stranger.

"You came to the right place. Among other things, I run a human being lost and found. Who are you looking for?"

"Me," he said.

"Come again?"

"Me," he said in a slightly louder voice.

I shook my head and laughed, wondering why I had to get a nut job on a busy night like this. The dark seemed to draw out the strange.

"I'm not joking, Mr. Moulton. I am looking for me because I've completely lost my memory." The slightest hint of worry crossed his face. "I have no idea who I am."

"You don't have any identification?"

"No."

"Why did you come to me? If you have amnesia, you need to see a doctor—a psychiatrist. I don't do headcases."

"No, no. A doctor might eventually bring in the authorities. I wouldn't want to risk that," he said.

"Why not?"

"The reason will come out in my story. Will you take my case? I can pay you."

"You have money in your wallet but no ID?"

"Will you listen to my story?" Impatience brought some life to his face.

"Sure, I'll take your case." Though I had no idea how I'd undertake a search such as this. "Please, go ahead and tell your story."

"My personal memory goes back only as far as last Monday night, which seems like a long time ago now. I found myself sitting on a downtown bench with a splitting headache, feeling as if I had just escaped from a horrible nightmare. But I couldn't figure out why I was sitting there. Then I realized the problem was even worse than that: I couldn't remember my name or what I did for a living. I immediately checked my pockets for a wallet, but nothing was there. All I found was a roll of money—with a lot of large bills. Did I bring it along, did someone give it to me, or did I take it away from someone? Of course, I couldn't answer that question." His big teeth bit into his lower lip.

"But what really alarmed me was the blood all over my jacket and tie. I wasn't bleeding anywhere, and so I told myself I must have been in a fight and bloodied the other guy. But then I started to worry that I had committed a crime that could be traced to me, whoever that was. Did I need to be running from the police? Thinking about that later, I recognized that I couldn't go see a respectable doctor: He would restore my memory and maybe uncover a crime that he was duty bound to report." He put his big hands on the edge of my desk with a grip that seemed poised for pushing.

"So you came to someone disrespectable—a private dick?"

He didn't—and maybe couldn't—laugh. "Don't you handle gray-area issues like this?"

"Well, I've never taken on a lost-memory case. But yes, dicks do work on the darker side of human relations, or as you call it, the gray-area issues. Where have you been holing up?"

"I've taken a room at the Milshire, a couple of blocks from

here. I sit there all day and all night, trying to gather my memory back. But it obviously hasn't worked, and so I thought I'd try you for help," he said in a matter-of-fact way.

"Where exactly were you when you discovered that your memory had taken a powder?"

"On the bus bench near the corner of Fifth and Marina."

"We should go down there together. It might help to return to the scene of the internal "crime"—your memory's abduction. Are you up for it now?"

"Yes. But let me pay you." He pulled out a wallet that looked newly bought to hold his bankroll. "How much do I owe you?"

"Two hundred dollars would be fine for now. But I might need more later." And in a case like this, it later looked as if it was going to come sooner. He put three hundreds on the desk. Green and fresh, they looked exactly like what my good health required.

"Sara, we need to take a short trip. See you later, dear."

"Okay, be careful, Matt." She knew nothing about the case, but she could smell the danger.

The murk that night was soupy, making driving more difficult than usual. I was glad that I hadn't been drinking.

The man took advantage of our short drive to further describe his loss on that night. "The funny thing was that I remembered everything else. I knew I was downtown in San Francisco, California. I knew what day, month, and year it was, and I even knew who the president of the United States was. But I couldn't remember a single solitary thing about myself."

"Wait a minute—I myself have forgotten who's president. Is it Truman?" I joked. Then I gave up: My humor just didn't work with a guy whose mind was so gone and whose manner was so dispassionate.

"Well, based on what I've seen and heard, I'd guess that you were reasonably well-educated and held a relatively powerful job directly impacting people," I said.

I also guessed that he was dangerous in some way, but I didn't want to upset him with that idea. He wasn't the kind of guy I'd want to encounter in the shadows.

"How in the world did you arrive at that?"

"The way you speak, the way you carry yourself, the looming aura you give off—they all say something about you."

"If only they'd tell you who I am," he said.

"That would make it all too easy. Now, where was your bench, on this side of the street or on the other side?"

"This side—over there."

"Maybe we can spark a single memory—anything would help you." We got out of the car near Fifth and Marina and walked to the bench. The now almost deserted downtown surrounded us.

I spotted a couple small drops of blood on the bench. "Look, could that be yours?"

"Yes, I was sitting on that side of the bench—it could be the blood from my coat."

"Was anyone else on the bench when you awoke?"

"No."

"Does being here again bring anything back?"

"I remember the strange, divided feeling I had that night. I was both confused about where I was and yet thoroughly acquainted with being there."

I felt like that a lot without any memory loss—two minds vying for one space. "Maybe your job was nearby, or you did a lot of work in the area."

"There's still no spark." He shook his head. "My mind is just a blank space when it comes to any personal history. How could it all have disappeared?" He brushed his hand through his hair and then left it there as if he were searching or conjuring or both.

"I don't know, but we'll work hard to bring it back, ah, John. May I call you John—John Doe? John V. Doe, for extra class?"

"I feel like a John Doe right now."

I looked around at all the tall buildings in the shadows of the night. That provoked a chilling thought: Just three blocks away lay the Woodward Building, where Barbara Martin was murdered. Could this guy have been involved in that? Could he have wandered over to this bench from there? That seemed like too much of a coincidence that the possible killer of my client's sister would come to me for help. Then again, maybe this guy killed Barbara Martin, and she wasn't Dorothy Worthington. It would still be a big problem for me. I wasn't too worried right now. I filed the idea away in my brain, but I left it in an open file.

"Have you seen enough, John?"

"Yes, more than enough."

"Let me drive you back to your hotel. But keep me in the know about any change in your condition, and I'll call you if I find out anything. What's your room number?"

"Seven-oh-seven."

Clients were always hiding important facts from me. But he was the first client who literally couldn't give me much of any information at all. I had nothing to work with. It was like playing a baseball game without balls, bats, gloves, and other players. All I could do was mime away alone on a wide-open field. How could I get to first base in such a case?

Chapter Six

The day after Doe didn't really begin until after dark. Sara had already gone home, but I remained at my desk, nursing a drink and waiting for Gina, who had just called. I looked forward to seeing her again—our last get-together reignited the old feelings. And I was eager to examine what she'd bring me regarding the Barbara Martin murder case.

The outer door opened, and I couldn't see who entered the reception office. But I knew it was Gina because I could detect her unique scent, which, if she bottled it, would probably be called something like Flowering Lust. She entered my office and smiled.

"Hello, sweetheart," I said.

"Good evening, Mr. Moulton." We kissed until we had to come up for air.

I pulled out the chair for her. "Please sit down. Would you like a drink?"

"No, but a cigarette would be nice."

I gave her one from my case and lit it for her. She took a long drag and wearily let out a waft of smoke. I sat down at my desk.

"I'm glad I caught you while you were still in the office," she said.

"If I'm not here, you can always reach me at home. You have

my number."

"Yes, but I don't want to interrupt your private life."

"Private life? What private life? You know I don't do much outside business. Lately my private life consists of thinking about you," I said, revealing more than I intended.

Her doubting grin almost turned into a gratified beam. Still, she said, "Yeah, and when does that happen, between servicing a blonde and a redhead?"

"Don't be cynical—it's all just business, sweetheart." I didn't mean to say that the way it sounded. But I was glad it came out that way because her possessive haughtiness needed a little brush back. You didn't want to let even loved ones get too close.

"Speaking of business, getting access to the Barbara Martin file was hard—sneaky hard. Brannigan kept it on his desk, and he stayed late every night, working past my quitting time. Today I decided to wait him out by doing overtime and reorganizing my files system. Finally, at 7:30, he told me he was going out for a half-hour bite and wanted me to listen for a call he was supposed to have gotten earlier in the evening. That gave me an excuse to be flitting in and out of his office.

"Once I was sure he was completely gone, I creeped into his office and searched the various piles of paper he had everywhere. I finally found the Martin file and took it back to my desk, where I stole through it, taking out and taking down as much information as I reasonably could. I had to interrupt my work when his call came in, and it used up valuable seconds that I didn't have. When I returned to the file, everything seemed to be working against me: a racing clock, sweating hands, aching nerves. Close to 8:00, I finally had to stop work and go return the file. Once I did that, I heard the outer door creak open, and I just knew that it had to be Brannigan. He's always so punctual."

"Oh, no! Then what did you do?

"I quickly picked up his phone and said 'thank you. I'll give him your message.' I acted as if I had just taken his precious call. I gave him the message and tore out of there. He just stared at me. My heart was pounding like a jazz drum solo."

"You're an effective sneak, sweetheart—you reacted quickly."

Those eyes were giving me a light slap. The hazel in them darkened a shade. "Don't go overboard with sweet compliments, Matt." The smiling eyes then returned.

"Oh yeah, right. Who's the investigating detective on the Martin case?"

"Bill Watson." He was the staff's one Negro detective.

"Why wasn't the file on Bill's desk?"

"Good question, but it's one I can't answer."

"Brannigan appears to be guarding that file. He would never give it to Bill, or anyone else for that matter. I'm surprised he didn't take it home with him. You would have been in big trouble if he had returned to his office and caught you with it. Honestly, I guess fate was on our side tonight."

"Fate, God, dumb luck—I'll accept help from any source. But I think that what I found will interest you. The file included many photos of the victim, and I brought you a couple duplicate copies. I also took notes of what seemed to be the most important information. I had to work fast and so the writing might not be very legible." She still seemed nervous as she handed me a large envelope with her self-created file.

The first thing I pulled out was a stunning photograph of Barbara Martin sprawled over a desk—a big wet spot covering the left side of her chest. Another photo closed in on Martin's pretty, heart-shaped face, and that one left me ninety-five percent certain the victim was Dorothy Worthington. Only the woman's closed eyes and convincing dark-hair dye job prevented me from going five percent further.

I was shaken—ninety-five percent certain was a pretty firm conclusion. "Forget Barbara Martin. This is actually my client's sister, a woman named Dorothy, who was due to inherit the Worthington fortune."

"Oh my God," she said, her jaw threatening to drop.

I read over Gina's scrawled notes until I encountered a line that really hit me where it hurts: "A four-year-old child, the victim's daughter, apparently witnessed the slaying." I put the notes down and closed the file. And then I just stared into space.

"There was a child at the murder site? Dorothy's daughter?" I asked out loud.

"I cried when I read that, though I had already heard people whispering about it throughout the department. I found photos of the little girl in the file, and I put one of them in your envelope," she said.

"But what was her little kid doing there, particularly late at night?" Knowing that Gina wouldn't know, I was addressing myself to the only one who would have the answer. The problem was that she had been permanently detained. I just felt that some questions had to be asked even when they were futile.

"The investigators didn't speculate. But maybe Barbara, or Dorothy, couldn't get a sitter that day and took the child along to work," said Gina. "Who knows?"

"And Dorothy was apparently working overtime into the night until...." I couldn't finish.

I felt defeated, deflated, depressed—and backed into a corner.

I would never find my client's sister. Meanwhile, I had to straighten out law enforcement about the real identity of the murder victim without exposing Gina's involvement with the file. And then there was the decency question: What will I do about Dorothy's daughter? Hell, what could I do? The worst already happened, as it too often does. The little girl is Amy's problem now.

I needed help, at least a cigarette or a drink. I opted for both.

"Would you like anything sweetheart?" I asked.

"I could go for a short drink."

I poured her one and said: "You broke my case, Gina, and now I think it's temporarily broken me."

"I'm sorry, Matt. But that seems to happen to you a lot in this business," she said, in an admonishing voice.

"You mean, you've noticed my pain before? I'm impressed." I got up, bent over, and kissed her. We talked a little more about the case and how we could keep her name out of it, and we traded a few suggestive pleasantries before I finally encouraged her to go home after her long day. I had things to do, starting with the delivery of the bad news to my client Amy.

I called the younger sister repeatedly that night, to no avail. I assumed that she was out exploring the town's many nightspots. What better chance would there be to spend a lot of money and show herself off at the same time? Sexless dispassion never looked sexier.

But the next day, I called all morning and afternoon and still couldn't reach her. It didn't make any sense that she wasn't in her hotel day or night. So, using my best anonymous city detective's voice, I called the Hilton and professionally demanded Amy Worthington's suite number. It was four-sixteen.

Seeking to avoid being seen, I walked up to the fourth floor and knocked on her door. Nothing. I knocked a second time and a third time, and still there was no answer or other sound of life. So I pulled out my handy paper clip, unbent it, and used it to jimmy her lock. I opened the door slowly, because I didn't want to inadvertently intrude on anything. But death doesn't care, it never minds at all, and that's what I found openly splaying on the floor: Death in the form of the head-bloodied body of once beautiful Amy Worthington. She was dressed for the night, but—tragically—it turns out she was going to sleep a lot longer than she had expected. I felt profoundly sad for Amy and Dorothy. But I also wondered how two sisters—the daughters of one of the richest men in America—both managed to get killed on my watch. I felt mad at myself as the most convenient target. I would have fired me.

I wanted to sit on her bed and puzzle my broken case together, but I didn't have time for that. I had to move quickly, checking out the entire suite for evidence and looking through her purse for what might be missing. Her money was still there, and so

the murder wasn't a robbery. I also noticed that my business card wasn't in her purse, though I didn't think anything of it at the time.

I slipped down the stairs and out of the hotel, then went to a pay phone to call the police. I reported hearing violent goings-on last night in room four-sixteen at the Hilton. When they asked for my name, I hung up the phone.

Next, I had to accomplish two things: Get confirmation of my Dorothy Worthington photos from someone with a professional eye and then find a way to alert law enforcement to the real identity of the Martin body. Only one person could help me with both, and that was Josh Baumberg, the veteran crime reporter at the Chronicle. I used him to strategically drop case information into the paper at least a half dozen times when I was a detective in the city bureau. He was always hankering for new material, and he was always working. Sleeping was for much later, when sleep was the only choice.

I went to the Chronicle and knocked on his open office door: "Hey Josh, do you have a couple minutes?" Wrinkled papers and open books cluttered his desk and every other above-the-floor surface in the room.

Josh Baumberg was a wise old journalist and an onion of a man: He had a head that was bulbous, a face that was cracked dry, and a manner that was sharp and even biting. He made people cry, too, but not in the usual onion-like way. He did it through thick and smelly smoke, the emission curling out of the cheap cigar butt perpetually planted in his round and parched little mouth.

"Hey Matt, where've you been keeping yourself? Come in, come in."

"Thanks, Josh." I removed a dog-eared open book from the guest chair and sat down.

"So you still dickin' around, Matt?"

"Sure, it more than pays the bills. But look, Josh, I have a question for you: Why haven't you guys paid more attention to the Barbara Martin slaying?"

"Ha! Not a fair question, Matt. I repeatedly tried to get information about that case from your old bureau, but it was no soap. They've closed themselves off about it. Well fuck them: I know they're covering something up." His infernal smoke brought tears to his little yellow eyes as well.

"Well Josh, I have information that may help us both. But you're to keep everything on the QT. You can't let my name get out as a source."

"Hey, wait a minute, have I ever exposed you before? I'm certainly not going to start doing it now."

"Okay, I'm glad we're straight about that." I pulled out the photo of Dorothy that Amy gave me. "This is a picture of my client's sister, the heir of the big Worthington fortune. Take a close look at it."

"The Worthington bundle? Okay, let me see. Oh yeah, nice face. But what about it?"

"Now let me show you crime photos of Barbara Martin. Look very closely." I handed them to him.

He looked at them from three vantage points, including up very close. "Hey, it's the same broad, but with different hair. Martin is Worthington. What a potential story!"

"That's what I thought, but I wasn't one hundred percent sure. How certain are you that they're the same woman?"

"Look, I'm not a hundred percent sure of anything at any time. Sometimes, after a few drinks, I'm not entirely sure I'm Josh Baumberg. But I'm as certain as I can be about my opinion on this one. I mean, what do you want me to do—sign a statement and get it notarized?"

I chuckled. "No, that won't be necessary, Josh. By the way, the crime file included the info that the victim's daughter, a four-year-old, was in the office at the time of the murder."

"Jesus, no," he pleaded. "The crimes keep getting worse—and more frequent."

"I agree Josh, and it's been true since the end of the war—I guess people get addicted to violence. The very worse may be yet to come. But look, here's the deal about the current problem: Though I can't let you have the Martin crime photos, I can give you my client picture of Dorothy. And then maybe you can write one of your speculative articles where you ask probing questions like "Why aren't the police looking into whether the murdered Barbara Martin was actually the missing Dorothy Worthington, heir to the Worthington fortune? They're the same age with the same face. You could even mention the kid in the article.

"You can get more information about Dorothy Worthington from Rita Slotkowski. That's Rita Slotkowski. She's in the San Francisco phone book. And for confirmation, show Dorothy's picture to Philbin at Philbin Accounting, the office next door to Martin's Worth Import/Export in the Woodward Building."

He exhaled a big puff of smoke. "I like it, I like it. You bring good stuff."

"The story will show how you're digging relentlessly for the truth, and it will put pressure on the cops to look into the Worthington angle on the body. Maybe they'll even call the family eventually. Right now, they're so buttoned up about all this that I don't think they really know who they've got on their hands. By writing your article, you can light a fire under Brannigan's ass to get something done."

He smiled, pointed his two cigar-stained fingers at me, and said, "Yeah, yeah, I like your imagery. It's a great place to light a fire. You ever think about writing yourself?"

"No, I can't even write a short sentence without screwing up. I'll leave the scribing to brainy guys like you." The smoke was starting to feel like razor blades cutting into my eyes, and so I moved to escape. "Thanks, Josh. Let me know if you need any more. And get that picture back to me in a day."

"What do you think, I'm going to keep it for my photo album? Yeah, yeah, so long, Matt!"

I hoped that, at the very least, a Baumberg news story would

46

put the little girl in a better position to be sent east, back to her family in Philadelphia. Now, though, the big question was about the girl's mother, Dorothy, and why her life ended so suddenly and violently.

Chapter Seven

I wanted to see how the other half lived—the half of Dorothy Worthington that was businesswoman Barbara Martin. So I headed out to her last known address on Palisades Drive in a slightly upper middle-class neighborhood on the city's south side. Her apartment building stood out on the block, giving class to the other aspiring buildings. It was sleekly new (ten years old or so), gaudily modernistic with all manner of gewgaws, and delicately colored in a shade of rose. Though it was the darkest part of night, I could clearly see that the building and the neighborhood were marked improvements over her first residential stop in San Francisco.

Worrying that Brannigan would have somebody watching over the place, I searched the block for people sitting in parked cars and looked up to make sure that Dorothy's fifth-floor apartment, at the top, was dark. I then went into the building through the back door, which was easier to jimmy. It was also a breeze getting into Dorothy's apartment, though I almost slipped and fell on a pull-along toy that was lying in the dark just inside the door. The place looked pleasant and comfortable, full of new and seemingly imported furniture that was more angular, colorful, and expensive than the typical mass-manufactured American kind. I wasn't going to find a

Sears catalog here.

Dorothy's little girl had her own room with all kinds of dolls and other toys carefully arranged in the corners. Some of those came from Europe as well. I put the pull-along toy back in there (where it would no longer be a safety hazard to prowlers).

When I entered Dorothy's room, I turned on the Tiffany lamp, intending to search for items that revealed or suggested something importantly personal. I went through her chest of drawers and then her dresser. In the bottom drawer of the latter, I encountered only a large but empty wooden case. It seemed as if someone had withdrawn its contents. And why did I suspect that that someone was a certain repressive and corrupt police detective?

I looked over everything again, combing the room, searching for any significant item, perhaps even a stray, pre-dyed, blonde hair. The last place I looked was under her bed and there I found it—something lying in the dark against the wall. I crawled underneath and grabbed it, and my prize ended up being two items loosely clipped together. They were photographs—color ones, no less. They portrayed Dorothy/Barbara with her arm romantically curled around a long-nosed, dark-haired man with olive skin and graying temples. His distinguished bearing looked vaguely familiar. The possibility of identifying him so nagged at me that I kept looking at the picture until my damn brain nearly broke: The guy was the mayor of San Francisco, Anthony Rossini. Dorothy was dating the city's chief elected official, presumably without a permission slip from his wife. Business had been good for Dorothy. She had been moving up on her own, perhaps with the help of a different kind of daddy.

I suspected that Brannigan's men ransacked the place, including the drawer with the now empty wooden case. They might have accidentally dropped it, with stuff splaying all over, including in places they couldn't see, like under the farthest part of the bed. In my mind, I thanked the lieutenant and his men for being so careless in spreading evidence they were trying to suppress.

After casting about a little more, I didn't think there was anything further I could learn, and I made my way out of there and drove off.

As I was heading home, I realized how drop-dead tired I was after a long and productive night. I looked forward to my little apartment, which was part of an eight-story former hotel. The two-room home was crisp, clean and quiet, a solid sanctuary from any screaming, crying, arguing, or lovemaking that might happen above me, below me, or next door. It was a place where I could escape and hide from a wild and ferocious world. When I pressed the elevator button to go to my floor, I remembered that I had left my envelope of notes and photos in the car, but I didn't have the energy to go back for it. "It's best if I leave it there," I told myself. "Work should stay in work."

I let myself into the apartment and turned on the light. When I turned around, I flinched upon discovering two uninvited guests, one holding a gun on me. All I could think of was, "So much for privacy." The chunky, unshaven gunsel in the baggy, bargain-basement suit patted me down and took the gun from the holster underneath my jacket. He didn't say a word.

"Welcome home, Mr. Moulton; we've been waiting for you awhile," said the mouthpiece, a tall but slight young man. His face was pretty, and his voice was soft, but the latter had a frightening edge to it. He could have been a nun out of habit. It reminded me of the bad old days of Catholic school.

"And who the Hell are you?"

"My name is Peter Worthington."

"Oh, yeah. Worthington, huh? I presume you're the one who murdered and defaced your sister Amy last night? That was brutal. What do you do to people who aren't family?"

His eyes virtually ceased activity, looking as dead as a couple of ink spots. He let out a sneer as an afterthought. "She was in the way."

"In the way of what?"

"Money, of course. Isn't that what we all want? Isn't that what you want, Mr. Moulton? I'm sure you insisted on being well compensated by Amy."

"Yes, we all want money. It makes the world turn. But I don't kill people for it. I wouldn't shoot my family for it. I'd let the world stop before I'd resort to such selfish shit."

"I guess you're a better human being than I am, Mr. Moulton."

"Well, do you mind if this supposed nice guy makes himself a drink?"

He laughed. "Go ahead," said Worthington.

"Don't try anything funny," growled the gunsel.

I crossed the room. "Is it too funny to ask if you gentlemen would like a drink?"

"No, we don't drink with people we don't know," said Worthington. This killer was a snob.

I poured a large one. I had needed a drink anyway, but now I was desperate for something. I gulped it down. I then picked up a handkerchief from the table and sat down on an easy chair facing the both of them. I conspicuously started wiping my face with the hanky. "It's getting hot in here," I said. It actually felt a little chilly.

Worthington giggled, leaving a most unpleasant impression. "Yeah, I imagine it must be getting a little warm for you." Even the gunsel looked askance at him.

I groused about my business card being in Amy's purse. This guy found it, stole it, and then broke into my fucking house, invading my space and threatening my life. I was furious, but I had to keep myself at a low boil for now.

"All we need from you, Mr. Moulton, is information. I assume Amy hired you to find Dorothy. Where is she? That's all we want to know and then we'll leave you alone." He sounded so reasonable.

"So you'll leave me alone after that?" Not a chance: They'll kill me whether I tell them anything or not. I was as good as dead. I wondered if my funeral would be well attended. Well, at least Gina and Sara would be there.

"Yes, we'll leave you alone, Mr. Moulton. We don't care about you—we want Dorothy."

I started wiping my face again. "But what are you going to do to Dorothy? Is she in the way, too?"

"That's none of your business, Mr. Moulton," he said in a voice now dripping with malice. He was getting impatient. And the gunsel looked nervous. "Did you leave anything lying around that could tell us about Dorothy's whereabouts?" said Worthington. He started looking here and there.

Worthington's sudden erratic movements distracted the gunsel ever so slightly—but it was just enough. I accidentally, on purpose, fumbled with my handkerchief and dropped it. Then, working as efficiently as I knew possible, I casually bent down to pick it up but reached for the holster under my pant cuff instead. I pulled out my derringer, aimed, and fired, hitting the astonished gunsel in the heart. I've been a marksman since I was a teen, and so this target wasn't a tough one. But I had no time to admire my work—I rushed to the body, withdrew the guns, and pointed my three helpmates at the young man without a heart. I patted Worthington down, though I didn't expect to find anything. I knew he didn't carry a gun or even know how to shoot one; he couldn't do anything for himself. For now, he was playing the weak, silent type, doing nothing more than shaking his head. He wouldn't talk without his attorneys.

"Well, what did you expect, Worthington? I guess you didn't do your homework about me. If you had, you would have known that I wasn't going to let you just walk into my home and murder me. Do you know me now?" I didn't like the guy, and it registered in my voice, which kept getting louder and harsher. "As a good dick, I prepare myself for crazy possibilities such as you. Just as you'll need to prepare yourself for the miserable probability of life in jail—if you're lucky and the jury ends up feeling sorry for you." I picked up the phone and dialed the police.

Four cops arrived and I was almost shocked to see they included Brannigan.

"When I got home, these two jokers were waiting with a drawn gun and promises to kill me. I finally had to shoot and kill the armed one—here's his gun. The other guy is a vicious pussycat who went around without a gun but was giving all the orders. His name is Peter Worthington, and he is part of an East Coast family that's worth millions. He killed his sister, my client Amy Worthington, last night in the San Francisco Hilton."

"How did you get mixed up with the Worthingtons, Moulton? They're way too rich for your blood, aren't they?" asked a grinning Brannigan in a mockingly serious voice.

"What's your question, Brannigan? Are you asking me what

kind of work I did for Amy? You know I don't have to answer that."

"For right now, I'm not asking you anything. But when I do have questions, you'd better have answers, Moulton."

"Speaking of questions, what are you doing here? Why are you still on the job so late?"

"What's it to you? I'm on a double shift. Unlike you, who spends every day posturing and troublemaking, I work for a living."

"Oh, is that what you call it?" It was hard to say whether my question rubbed Brannigan the wrong way since everything that came out of my mouth, especially mere breath, seemed to antagonize him. But he did look as if he were ready to kill me.

"Go ahead, Moulton, keep pushing. One day, you'll say the wrong thing or take the wrong step, and you'll pay dearly. Okay, guys, let's clear out." The detectives took hold of Worthington, and the paramedics carried out his stooge.

I was relieved that the night was ending—it could easily have been the last one of my life. But I regretted the consequence of the police call, no matter how necessary it was. Brannigan now knew that I was involved with the Worthingtons, and that meant that when the Chronicle article about Dorothy hit the streets, he was going to assume that I was the source for it. And he would probably suspect Gina as well. How angry he got about the story would depend on what he was covering up in the Barbara Martin/Dorothy Worthington murder. If it was something truly major, Gina and I would be in serious trouble with him. But I couldn't stop a newshound like Baumberg from publishing now that I sparked his own suspicions.

Of course, I was suspicious about not only Brannigan but also John Doe. Why did I keep worrying that my mindless client was somehow involved with the Worthington case?

Chapter Eight

Forget about municipal law or Brannigan's Law. What too often governs a private dick's most complicated cases is the Law of Diminishing Returns, which ensures that the more you learn, the less you'll know, or at least understand. A tough case can feel like time going backwards, with your goal—reaching the end and the truth—gradually and perpetually fading from view. The Worthington case, unfortunately, obeyed that law, or—at least—it seemed that way after a long night of revelation and riddle.

But I couldn't stop digging for the answers. I owed it to Amy to find out what happened to her sister. And I owed it to John Doe to help him recover his identity. Were the two cases related? I increasingly thought they could be, and so I asked John to stop by the office.

While I waited for him, I struggled with the new Chronicle article that questioned whether Barbara Martin was really a Worthington heir named Dorothy. It was the well-written front-page story that I had wanted to see, but now it represented a potential problem.

Sara buzzed me on the intercom. "Matt, John's here."

"Thanks, dearie, send him in."

John Doe entered silently with his characteristic economy of movement and expression. However, I knew him well enough by this time to recognize a subtle sign of trouble in his eyes and in his whole manner. Losing a mind can be wearing on a person. And it didn't help that he still hadn't bought a change of clothes.

"Hi, John, please take a seat." He took off his hat and coat and placed them on the second chair. He then sat down in the first one.

He still hadn't said a word. "Have you recovered a shred of personal memory?"

"No."

"Is there anything more about the first night that you remember?"

"No."

"Well, I wanted to show you a few things related to another case I'm working on. I don't know what makes me think you'd know anything about them. Call it a hunch. But if it's a good hunch, it could help you and help me."

He continued to look at me with an expression of pained detachment.

I handed him a picture of Dorothy Worthington. "I've been looking for this woman. She's my client's sister, the heir to the Worthington fortune."

He looked it over closely for a few seconds. "She doesn't spark any memories."

I showed him the photo of the slain woman. "This was a victim named Barbara Martin, but I think she's actually Dorothy Worthington. She was killed downtown on the night you woke up on that bus bench. It happened just three blocks away."

He stared at the picture and seemed to show a sign of distant recognition. He then closed his eyes and desperately fingered them as if they had started to burn or play other tricks on him.

"Anything wrong, John?"

"I think I was looking for too long."

"Did you recognize or remember anything?"

"Something about that picture seems familiar. Was it in the newspaper?"

"No, the detective bureau has largely kept the story out of the papers. You're one of the few people who have seen the picture. Do you recognize the woman?"

"I feel as if I've seen her before."

I brought out the picture of Dorothy's daughter. "Unfortunately, the victim's daughter witnessed the murder. This is she, a four-year-old."

He looked at the photo and this time something painfully specific came to him. In fact, if it was a memory, it seemed to be attacking him, wrinkling and finally distorting his face, shutting his eyes, and forcing a moan through his lips. "Noooh, noooh," he cried, again and again as he reopened his eyes and peered at the picture. Then he dropped the photo as the memory struck his ears, which he covered with his hands, as if it carried a deafening sound. It began to choke him, his breaths coming only in great gasps. Finally, this invisible monster wiped him out, forced him to collapse out of the chair, and just fold up in front of me. The big man virtually shrunk. It was frightening to witness. I thought the attack had killed him for sure.

I was wrong—he was still breathing. I dragged him over to the sofa in the corner of the room and carefully uncoiled him. He had the bleached pale look of a dead man before his funeral make-up.

I called Sara. "John just fainted. Do we have any smelling

salts?"

"Oh sure, Matt. I'll bring them in."

She waved the open bottle under his nose again and again, and we waited. First, he started to breathe heavily. Then his eyelids began to flutter, and his mouth began to open. Finally, something emerged in a garbled voice, "My head…my head… my head is killing me."

"No problem, John. Sara will get you some aspirin. We run a drug store here on the side."

After he swallowed the aspirin and water, I asked him if he wanted a drink. He surprised me by saying yes, and I needed to join him.

Once everything settled down, he moaned a little more and then finally slurred, "Thanks, Matt. I'm starting to get memories. They're blurry, but I can start to make them out and understand them." His mouth tried taking the form of a smile.

"Really? They sure acted unfriendly at first. If that's the way lost memories return, I might choose to do without them. Forgetting is more forgiving…."

I think he responded with, "I feel so much better having some idea of who I am. It's a real relief already." It sounded like he said, "Weel relief."

I let him lie there and try to focus his mind. His expression suggested that it was a painful process.

About a half hour later, I said, "Can you begin to tell your story? Do you know who you are, where you grew up, who your parents are?

"I grew up here, in San Francisco. And I remember my mom and…the father." The last two words sounded almost like a barb, but maybe it was just slurred speech.

"Who are you, and what do you do for a living?"

He went mute, acting as if he didn't want to tell me a thing.

"Look, nothing you tell me goes beyond this room. It's completely confidential. And you can trust Sara as much as you can trust me—she's my partner." I was pacing around, and Sara was on the edge of her chair.

He was quiet for another minute, and then he said, "Well, my name really is John—John Boorman. But I use a number of aliases."

"Oh, of course, doesn't everyone? Now what do you do? What's your business?"

"I've never actually...told anyone before." He started to sound fully intelligible. The hangover from the attack appeared to be dissipating.

"Well, I assume you've never actually lost your memory before, and you've never actually hired a gumshoe before. This is an unusual situation."

"Let's see, how can I put it? I need to find the words." He was silent for seconds more. "Well, I killed people for a living." Sara gasped, and I probably did the facial equivalent of that.

"You were a paid assassin?" I asked.

"I don't know if I like that term. What I actually did was provide an expert service for a price." I could tell he was recovered—he was skillfully trying to whitewash his work, give it a corporate gleam.

"I used to see my job as just a roughshod form of capitalism. I was doing for people what they couldn't do on their own."

"It sounds as if you're trying to justify it. All I want to know is what you did for a living. In your business, you eliminated people."

"Exactly. I got rid of husbands, wives, business partners, business competitors, relatives, politicians. To clients, they were just inconvenient people. In one case, a guy wanted his son taken out." That was supposed to be an extreme example, but he delivered it in such a matter-of-fact voice that it sounded like business as usual. Simply keeping violence in the family.

"Why?"

"He felt that his son was going to take his business and money away."

I couldn't help myself. "Jesus John, didn't the foul nature of such work bother you? Cause you any sleepless nights?"

John sat up, clenched his mouth, and tucked in his chin. "It did in the beginning. I always felt upset about it. It didn't seem right to have all that power." He tightened his tie in apology.

"But after eliminating several people, it started to become just a job, just a way of earning big money. To tell the truth, I became kind of proud of my work—I always did a lot of careful research before I targeted people." He sat up and looked twice as intimidating.

"I'd learn where they lived and worked and played, who they spent time with, what their schedules and habits were. I'd do an entire profile on a target before I'd plan the hit. It would help me determine when and how I'd—well—kill the person. As to the how, much of the time I'd use a gun, but sometimes a knife or even an untraceable poison would be the best device. I always— well, almost always—did my job well." As if to eliminate his own doubts about competence, he swallowed hard for emphasis.

"Wait. There's an untraceable poison?"

"It has worked that way so far. The last time I used it was to eliminate a city council member for an incredibly wealthy client, one of his colleagues. You need to be careful with political murders because they attract so much attention from the press. This job practically demanded a subtle solution like poison because the client—a businessman outside his council job—was a vehemently vocal political opponent of the target. If I had shot him, it would have been an obvious murder, and everyone would have been buzzing about the rich guy somehow being responsible. So instead I got a job on the staff that was catering a big political dinner that included both men. I maneuvered my way into the position of preparing the individual plates, and I was able to sprinkle the target's dish with the tasteless, colorless poison. It didn't work right away. The guy died at home a little while later, seemingly of a heart attack. The poison was a quietly effective killer, salt with a fatal kick. It earned me a bonus for that job." He started to smile, but then thought better of it. Sara and I wouldn't have been a sympathetic audience.

"I always had to be creative. Once, when my target was a businessman/husband, I took advantage of the fact that he was rebuilding the family's second home. I secretly removed the supports from his false first floor, and it collapsed the next time he stepped on it. He took a long, apparently head-first fall into the unfinished basement and died. Of course, there was never a news story or cursory police investigation—because it seemed to be just an accident. It was the perfect solution for a hit." He just couldn't suppress the pride.

"Sounds like you knew a lot about building—or at least destroying—homes."

"Not really. I just had to learn how to wear many hats. Each job seemed to require a couple different ones."

"Did people approach you directly—er, hats in hand—about killing somebody?"

He aborted any smile and stuck to the facts. "Oh, no. I got all my work through a guy named Chance Diamond."

"Yes, I've heard of him. He's a kind of independent crime

figure, isn't he?"

"Yes, he's organized crime, but it's strictly his organization. When I returned from the war in the Pacific, I was rootless and restless. I couldn't see myself returning to the quiet life of college after going through the bloody mess of constant battle. I felt lost, and I didn't have anyone to guide me along into something. It seemed impossible to start out on a career. I mostly hung around in pool halls and gambling joints and eventually fell under the wing of Chance, who was very nice to me, like a father, a real one." He really raised his voice on real. "Chance gave me a lot of confidence. He kept telling me he saw great things ahead for me, and he eventually, gradually persuaded me to become one of his hit men."

Boorman's biography made me uneasy because it was somewhat like mine. I, too, went to college before the war, except I finished my degree. Unlike him, I had a purpose after school: I fully intended to write for the press, like my dad did, or manage a business, like my grandfather did. But the war changed everything for me, too. I didn't become addicted to the action and excitement of battle, as seemed to be the case with John. But what I saw as my secretly sinister activity in the war sentenced me to the darker side of life when it came to a permanent career. What else was I suited to do? If it wasn't emotionally messy and physically dangerous, if it didn't involve people often acting at their worst, then it apparently wasn't for me. "John, you're saying there are other hitmen in Chance's group?"

"Yes, contract killing is a thriving business. Chance acts as a kind of screen for all the requests: He determines if the client has the money for the job and whether he or she has something to lose if things go wrong. The system would collapse if a client suddenly got cold feet and went to the press or the police.

Chance's screening process prevents that and ensures that he gets the wealthiest trade—he runs a kind of VIP Murders, Inc."

"What about the police? How does Diamond handle them in cases that strongly suggest murder?"

"Several policemen are part of the team. Chance works with them through Lieutenant Gilbert Brannigan."

"What!? Brannigan? Brannigan!"

"Yes, he gets a percentage of each job, and then he presumably shares the money with his officers. It's a pretty lucrative commission."

"My God! I used to work for him. I knew he was corrupt, but I didn't know his crookedness went as far as contracted murder." Brannigan as part of a hit squad made sense, but it seemed almost too true to be real.

"Chance couldn't run that business without the cooperation of the police. Brannigan is indispensable—he's part of the team."

"How high does this official involvement go? Is Chief of Police O'Brien involved?"

He was quiet for a few seconds as if he were trying to frame the answer. "Ah, that I don't know. All I can tell you about for sure is Brannigan's role."

Sara and I looked at each other with mutual sadness. Though we both knew about a lot of official corruption, we never imagined that law and order in San Francisco had become that dirty and sleazy.

"Okay, John, I think the time has arrived to tell us about your most recent job—the one that got me involved."

Chapter Nine

I lost a client and her sister, both to murder. I antagonized a brutal and corrupt police lieutenant with a press leak. Now a hitman, also my client, was about to explain the role he played in all that had gone wrong. Why wasn't I looking forward to this story? It was getting too personal.

"I had been delivering big on a lot of hits. So I wasn't surprised when Chance came to me with an important job—eliminating a downtown businesswoman named Barbara Martin," Boorman said.

"What made this one so important? I asked.

"It was the client. We got the assignment from the mayor of San Francisco."

"The mayor!?"

"Yes, that's right. He had been dating Martin for years, and they'd even had a child together. But according to the mayor, she had always accepted that he could never leave his wife—until a few months ago. Then supposedly, she had started pressuring him to change his life, give up his public office, and leave his wife for her. The mayor hated that pressure and what he claimed was the threat of blackmail, and so he decided to get rid of her."

"He asked you—through Chance—to kill his daughter's

mother?"

"Yes," he said with some reluctance.

"And what would happen to his daughter?"

"Beats me. He didn't say, but I guess he assumed she'd be placed somewhere, in a foster home or something."

"Did he know that Barbara Martin was actually Dorothy Worthington? Did you know?"

"I didn't know, and I don't think he did either. Frankly, considering what I've heard about him, I don't believe he would have targeted Martin if he had known that she was heir to the Worthington fortune. Big money would have been a big factor in her favor, despite his marriage and high office."

I could only smile and shake my head. "Unfortunately, you're probably right, John." He started to talk again, but I interrupted. "While we're piling on the mayor, we also need to carefully consider Dorothy Worthington. As Barbara Martin, she wouldn't have blackmailed his honor—she didn't have the personality for it. I'm betting he lied about blackmail to justify the hit."

Boorman just looked at me. "He wouldn't be the first hit client to lie.

"But as to his job itself, I screwed up terribly—I wasn't even a good bad guy in this case despite all my careful planning. I knew exactly how far she sat from the office door. My plan was to shoot her from there and avoid any blood splattering on me. However, when I walked in, she was standing just inside the door in front of her desk. Her pretty face was practically in mine. I panicked and shot right away, and her blood splattered all over my jacket. She slowly fell backwards.

"The situation plunged downhill from there. Suddenly I heard the cry 'mommy,' and I saw this little girl scamper to

Martin's side from under a nearby desk, where I guess she had been playing. Of course, I knew she had a daughter; what I didn't expect was that the lousy kid would be in the office that night to witness my killing her mother. She climbed on top of the desk and tried desperately to soothe and revive her mom. She kept crying 'mommy, mommy.'" He choked on what he wanted to say next.

After a few uncertain seconds, he seemed to barely regain his composure. "It was a tragic sight. I felt as horrible as if I had killed the little girl herself." His eyes started to blink compulsively, and sweat beads broke out all over his face. His conscience was still punishing him, still lashing away.

"All my targets had innocent family connections, but I was always able to keep them out of it. Not this time." His last words barely escaped.

"I was so upset that—for a hot minute—I even contemplated killing myself," he said, addressing himself to the floor, an uncritical but unsympathetic audience. "I'm being honest about that. But my selfishness and sense of survival took over: I wiped the gun clean of fingerprints and threw it down the floor's garbage shaft. Then, I took an elevator down and left the building. My intention was to walk a block and then catch a cab, but I just kept walking and walking until I could no longer continue. I crumpled over on that bench, and when I woke up sometime later, I had completely lost myself—my mind was gone." He shook his head and buried his chin into his chest.

"John, why didn't you carry an ID with you? Even a fake one might have jogged your memory."

He rolled his eyes as if he didn't want to talk any longer. "I never take an ID with me on a job. If I'm arrested, I'm free to make up any name or address. That flexibility protects me and the organization. Besides, I wasn't planning on possibly needing to revive my memory."

Hearing his story caused me great pain. First and foremost, of course, I grieved about Dorothy's girl. But I also started feeling bad about my past as a kind of hitman. My own guilt was on the ground, and it made me almost physically ill.

"John, though you were late and selective in recognizing the foul nature of what you did for a living, I can still identify with your discomfort in a general way. You see, I, too, worked as a kind of sniper or assassin. The difference was that I didn't report to the mob—my boss was Uncle Sam in German-occupied Vichy France. I feel as if I've done your kind of work."

Boorman lifted his head and looked at me with an expression that fell well short of surprise.

"Oh c'mon Matt, that's ridiculous. There's no comparison between the two," said Sara, dismissing me with a smile and a handwave. "You were killing bad guys, and your work helped put a quicker end to the war. Fewer Americans died as a result."

"Sara, I'll concede you all of that. And I know one thing: I never killed a German officer or a Gestapo agent in front of little kids. But I still felt that what I was doing was dishonorable and wrong. Instead of standing on the other side of some invisible line and shooting it out with the bad guys, with the best or the luckiest shots winning the day, I was sneaking around and killing people from secret hiding places. Courage? I should have gotten a medal for secrecy and safety.

"I found it hard to live day-to-day with the fact of being a sniper. Yes, I dispatched horrible people, but some of my targets were just career military officers and draftees. They weren't all Nazis—some deserved the chance to defend their lives in open battle."

The past was getting me all worked up again. Like some weak-minded idiot, I suddenly felt in a confessional mood. "I had to kill a general who was one of the leaders of the German Occupied Forces in France. Coming from a rural background, he loved to mingle with the farmers and their animals in Vichy, and that left him foolishly wide open as a target. The French Underground received intelligence that he was visiting this huge horse farm in the South, and so I headed out there with a couple of spotters, mixing in as part of the French-speaking hired help. Soon, we caught him alone, unarmed and out of uniform, with his beloved animals. But German soldiers virtually surrounded the complex, so I couldn't do anything as noisily obvious as shooting him. I had to kill him with a knife, and—it turned out—a much too dull one at that.

"When he went into a stable to spend time with his favorite horse, a pure white beauty named Blanche, I followed him. The sound of my footsteps crunching through the grain and dried hay exposed me, and he turned around. But the knife was hidden in my leg pocket, and he assumed I was just another Gaston or Pierre coming to tend to the animals.

"He turned back toward Blanche and started stroking her, telling her in broken French how sweet and beautiful she was. As he kept gently stroking and petting her, I pulled out the knife and plunged it forward. He turned to say something to me about Blanche and moved his body enough so that the knife drove into his side instead of his back. The blood spurted like thick red water from a twisted backyard hose. He looked horrified and stared at me. He tried to talk, but only muffled whispers came out of his wide-open mouth. Despite the labored breathing and fading voice, he refused to fall and refused to die. He just stood there. And so I yanked the knife from his side and wrenched it into his gut.

"He still just stood there, taunting me with whispered gurgles. I felt desperate. Not knowing what else to do, I belted him in the face. He fell backwards next to Blanche, but he still refused to stop breathing. He kept mouthing words I couldn't understand. He just bled and pled, bled and pled. But I couldn't just leave him there in that state. I bent over, put my hands around his neck, and squeezed and squeezed and squeezed as he gaped at me with begging, bulging eyes and flaccid lips. It took forever and ever, my hands were going numb, but the life in him finally and reluctantly surrendered as blood and saliva and vomit gushed out of his mouth.

"His reaction of shock, disappointment, fear, and perhaps regret—suggesting that his emotional hurt was greater than his physical pain—was so human that I forgot he was the enemy." I shook my head. "He could have been the most vicious killer in the world, but he hadn't done anything wrong to me. And yet I sneakily snuffed him out, torturing him in the process. I then wiped my bloody and pukey hands in his shirt, buried him in the hay and the horseshit, and quickly slipped out of there into the moonless, starless night.

"It was hard for me to eat, drink, or sleep for a long while afterwards. Assignments such as that made me feel disgusted about a war that everybody was calling just. Sometimes, it seemed to be *just*—*just* officially approved violence on both sides, like all wars were. It was nothing uplifting and heroic, at least not when it came to my role in the death match."

Even after all this time, the memory brought back a feeling of nausea, a mental or spiritual kind. "I don't know, John, but I guess your story reminded me of how guilty I am, or at least how guilty I feel. Call me soft, but your case brings back an old problem for me—targeting individual people for death."

"I'm a moral pygmy, and so I don't have a right to judge anybody," he said as he regained the ability to swallow—at least that statement, anyway. "But I think that you're being way too tough on yourself for being an assassin in war. Sara's right, it's not the same thing as what I've done."

I found it hard to accept that kind of moral reasoning from someone like Boorman. Besides, his loss of memory was what brought mine back, and now I was suffering anew for it. I wished he would just shut the fuck up about the whole subject. But stopping the discussion had to start with me.

"Thank you, John, but I think we've exhausted the angle of the 'hit man's guilt.' Besides, it looks as if we're not going to be able to agree on the morality of assassination. We now have to look to the future and—specifically—what we're going to do about Gilbert Brannigan and Chance Diamond."

"I guarantee you that Chance is very displeased with me. Consider why: I disappeared after the Martin hit—I didn't report back to him. He no doubt fears that I'm either talking to someone or getting ready to."

"Yes, this morning's Chronicle story probably just worried him a lot more. The article introduces the Martin case to the public and brings the Worthington name into the picture. It's unwanted publicity for a Diamond-assigned murder. So, in his mind, part of the solution to the problem may be getting rid of you."

One of the whitest men in the world turned paler. "I didn't know about that story. That's terrible news for me," he said.

"I planted the story, but it's terrible news for me, too. Not only can Brannigan read, at least when mouthing the words, but he can also remember my connection with the Worthingtons as both their personal gumshoe and a near-murder victim of the younger brother last night. He knows that I know he's covering up your hit."

I continued: "But if Brannigan and I and you and Diamond are at odds, that's nothing compared to the current relationship between Brannigan and Diamond. If his press-weary bosses order him to act, Detective Brannigan will have to go after Diamond, and Diamond knows it. If arrested, will he then betray Brannigan? I'm guessing that the two are almost drowning in pools of mutual suspicion. Maybe we can think of a way of taking advantage of that. Our lives may depend upon it."

"Whatever we do about them, I'll soon need to leave San Francisco for good," he said.

"Oh, of course, there's no question about that. But if I were you, for now I'd continue to stay at the Milshire. I wouldn't return to your home for anything—it's surely being watched. In the meantime, I'll think about where we can put you permanently. Do you like Europe?"

"Does it have to be so far away?"

He was incredibly naïve for a hardcore hitman. "Well, let's see, you committed how many felony murders? And you say the perception on the street is that you crossed Chance Diamond, your mobbed-up boss? It's not possible for you to move too far away from here, my friend. Even Europe may be too close!"

"I guess you're right." He took out his wallet. "Meanwhile, I owe you some more money for the work you've done." He removed five one-hundred-dollar bills. "Is this enough?"

"Thanks, John. It doesn't pay the piper, but it more than meets my part of the bill. I'll call you in a day or so. Please let us know if anything out of the ordinary happens. Be careful."

As Boorman and his recovered mind left, Sara looked into my eyes and opened her mouth to say something. An "ah" emerged and nothing more. She then looked at the floor, closed her eyes, shook her head, and returned to the outer office. The developments of the last few hours rendered her mute. Life could do that to other people, but never Sara, until now.

Meanwhile, I headed for the bottle. A couple of stiff drinks wouldn't protect me from any coming danger, nor would they help me wrestle with my painful war guilt, but they might quiet my fears of both. And on this dark day, I needed that more than anything else in the world.

Chapter Ten

The lights were out, and the heat was on, but the world kept turning. Though I was in an impossibly perilous position with the Worthington case, I had other clients to serve, other cases to solve. I spent the rest of the day working on a couple of urgent philandering husband cases, mainly planning when and how to use photography to catch the guys with their pants down. Balconies, fire escapes, hotel rooms next door, and rooms across the street could all play important roles. Of course, I also needed hotel cooperation. I didn't like that kind of work because it was too easy. But it paid the bills—and then some.

Around about seven in the evening, my stomach started to growl from hunger. It tended to get ornery like that, demanding food at least once every day. So I decided to head to my favorite diner, which was a couple blocks away from the office.

"Hey Sara, do you want to join me for dinner at Nick's?"

"No thanks, Matt. I'm expecting a call in the next half hour. I brought a sandwich from home."

"Okay, doll, I can take a hint. But don't hang around this dreary place too long. See you tomorrow."

She laughed and waved me off.

I left the building in a mental fog that seemed to take an

appropriately physical form outside. It was a struggle to see through all that haze. For a half block, the Palace Theater broke through with bright marquee light, advertising a new movie called "White Heat" with James Cagney. I couldn't help stopping to look at the movie's sensationalistic poster. Though I liked crime movies like that, I found that they were often a little too tame, a little too simple-minded. But maybe that was just me—a bias I formed from the harshly real world in which I did business. Once I passed the Palace, that real-world returned.

Across the street, I saw a tall man signaling to someone. Oddly, he looked and carried himself like Brannigan, but the fog so clouded his features that I couldn't be positive it was him at first. As I was crossing the alley, someone knocked me to the ground from behind. My head hit the fender of a parked car. A dark-suited guy then repeatedly kicked me in the puss and the gut with pointy, shiny black shoes, driving me deeper into the alley. A second lighter-suited guy, who seemed as massive as the most overfed football player, lifted me up and almost took my head off with a wild swing of his fist. I hit the jaggedy concrete again, and this fall hurt a lot more than the last one. That apparently inspired the other guy to bend over and pummel me, many of his punches landing in my angry, empty belly. There was nothing there to allow me the luxurious release of throwing up.

I wanted to reach for one of my guns, but the relentlessness of their pounding fists and booting feet made that almost impossible. Who were these violent clowns? Were they Brannigan's detectives or merely Brannigan's hired thugs? Why did I care about that when I was crippled with pain and threatened with death? That became a moot point as soon as the pointy-shoed guy picked up a couple of garbage can lids and banged them together—with my head in the middle. I could no longer hear, much less think. My head felt like a mashed potato in an echo chamber. But it wasn't over quite yet: As I was trying to reach for the gun under my jacket, the big guy delivered another roundhouse to my face. I fell to the ground and plunged into the black.

When I awoke, I knew where I was and who was ministering to me. The question was why: Why was Sara dabbing alcohol on my face as I lay on the couch in the office? And why did my body feel as if it were broken in a thousand pieces and held together only by the now scummy and tattered clothes wrapped around me? It was real surrealism.

"Thank God you're back. How do you feel, Matt?"

"Like an abandoned mine."

"When you didn't return from Nick's, I went out looking for you and found your moaning body lying in an alley. I wanted to call an ambulance, but I knew you'd never forgive me for doing that, and so I went to Nick's for help. Bob Wang was there, and he carried you to his car and drove us back to the office."

"Thank goodness for Bob—he's a big boy."

"He had to be—you were dead heavy."

"What does my face look like?"

"Well, it's cut, battered, and badly bruised. You look awful."

With those words, my feeling memory returned. I started to recall what happened in the gloom of that alley. "Well, I guess you can thank Brannigan for that."

"Oh no, what happened?"

I knew the words, but my mouth had a hard time forming and uttering them. "I thought I saw him signaling to someone from across the street...and then suddenly two goons jumped

76

me from behind. They gave me the beating of a lifetime. Then one of them coldcocked me. But was it a warning, or was it supposed to be my finish?"

"I'll bet it was a warning," she said. "Why would Brannigan murder you in an alley just off a busy street one block or so from your office? It was too risky—too many possible witnesses."

"Yeah, that's what I thought, too. But as brutal as these two guys were, they were obvious amateurs. There was no subtlety in their work. I see them as guys who would either do too much or too little, the latter being true if they were supposed to kill me. But you're right; they were probably delivering a warning. It almost went too far."

"What will you do now?"

"Be more careful, for one thing. And for another, worry about Gina. Now that Brannigan's connected me with the Worthington news leak, he surely suspects that Gina helped get me the information. I'll have to warn her to watch her step."

"I'm worried for you both."

"Maybe there's a way out of it. I'll need to meet with Boorman again tomorrow. Can you arrange it?"

"Of course. What are you doing?"

"Just the impossible, like trying to stand up. But don't help me, Sara—I've got to do it on my own." I felt like a hundred-year-old man who had fallen down a flight of concrete stairs—face first.

I limped over to the mirror next to the window, and I hated what it showed me. My face was in a state of discolored disorder—bulging black eye here, disjointed and blue-bruised cheekbone there. It would have been almost pathetic without the flashing movie light, which lent my face a downright sinister quality. Was that really me? I didn't have time to worry about it.

"Sara, I'm going home for the night."

"I can drive you home, Matt."

"No thanks, doll—you've done enough. I already owe you for rescuing me. How much more debt do you want me to carry?"

"Well, be very, very careful, Matt."

"Sure, I plan to live a little while longer. Later, Sara."

Over the next hour, I felt I conquered the world because I was able to shuffle off to my car, drive it a few blocks through light traffic, get into my apartment without someone's fist in my face or gun in my back, and take a laborious but luxurious bath. What other great things could I accomplish? I could think of only one important thing more.

I drove to the modest, black-and-white apartment building and parked directly in front. It was in a family-oriented neighborhood, but it was so late at night that there was no one on the street roaming around. My paper clip opened the outside door, and the stairs took me up to the third floor. It was much too late, but I knocked on the door.

"Who's there? she asked nervously.

"Gina, it's Matt."

"Matt, I'm not dressed."

"Well, put something on, sweetheart—I have to see you. It's important."

She opened the door, revealing a sweet doll on the verge of going to bed. There was no makeup on her face, and only a bra and panties barely covered the rest of her. She was beautiful, and I loved rediscovering it without the embellishments.

She didn't have to say a word; her eyes expressed the shock. But she nevertheless cried: "Oh my goodness, Matt, what's happened to you? Are you okay?" She touched my face and lightly patted and caressed it, and then she helped me over to the large, comfortable pillows of her beige sofa.

"It appears I ran into your boss, specifically his henchmen."

"Brannigan? Brannigan did this to you? Why?"

"I don't know—how do you explain crazy? My best answer is that he fears what I know about the Barbara Martin case."

"He fears that you simply know about it?"

"No, it's much more than that. I don't want to scare you with all the grimy details, but Martin—my client's sister Dorothy Worthington—was murdered with Brannigan's knowledge and perhaps approval. If that got out, he'd go to jail, and the chair could be his final resting place. Of course, he must find a way to keep me quiet, permanently."

"Even I didn't think that he was capable of stooping so low," she said.

"He's a snake. But I'm not so concerned about what he could do to me—I'm more worried about your safety. How has he been treating you since you messed with his file?"

"Unless I'm imagining things, it feels like he's been more openly dismissive of me lately."

"Gina, heed your suspicions. Never trust him. Don't walk alone anywhere. Stay away from the police outside the office. Consider them your enemy. I might have to drive you around from now on."

She sat up on her knees and put her hands on her hips. "Are you crazy? I won't let you be my combination body-guard/babysitter. I'm an adult who can take care of herself."

"Don't get offended, sweetheart. I just want to keep you from being hurt or even killed."

I lightly kissed her eyes, her nose, her mouth. She responded by burying her lips in mine, violating our unspoken agreement to dial back the passion. We ended up in a fully prone embrace, and—despite my burning face and aching body—I then raised the intensity. I gingerly lowered my body, slipped off her panties, and started caressing and kissing her other lips. She moaned. It was purely improvisational—beautiful music to my ears.

There was no going back now. I stood up and started peeling off my clothes—it only took half the night. Once I was finished, she took my hand and led me into her bedroom. She eased me down into her unmade bed, removed her bra, kissed my chest, and gently mounted me. She understood that if this was going to be our night of lust and love, she would have to lead it with the greater physical effort. I hated the idea, but I loved the result. We really found a rhythm together. We could feel the music.

After we made love, we spent an hour or so snuggling in bed, sweet-talking and wisecracking, a mix that had been typical of our relationship in its early days. But it was hard to stay carefree with the prospect of a lawless lawman looming over you. We started mildly arguing about who faced the greater danger from him. I pushed hard on her vulnerability as his female underling. She sent the argument back to me with her own good point. "You're right, and he's wrong, but he's the police, and so you have to be careful where you step. Don't antagonize him!"

"I'll be careful to antagonize him in just the right way. But I better get something to eat first, to avoid antagonizing my stomach. I don't want to keep you up too much longer, but do you have anything left in your fridge?"

"Oh, no. I'll bet you haven't eaten anything today."

"You'd win that one big, babydoll."

80

She left the bed and—to my great disappointment—covered herself up in a robe. "I'll go make you some eggs and bacon. You want orange juice, too, Matt?" I usually didn't have a stomach for such outward expressions of domesticity, but my hunger welcomed it now—my belly being as empty as a beggar man's pockets. I could only marvel at what a sweet night it had become after that bitter beginning.

Chapter Eleven

When I returned to the office the next day, I felt like a new man—or at least I almost did. I was still walking in pain, though I no longer felt crippled. My face showed improvement: I now looked like a million bucks—that had been partially burned in a fire. Everything seemed rosier because I had had a great late night with Gina.

But then my mind took over—critical thinking returned. Brannigan and Diamond would make it impossible to work and difficult to live. They were problems that Boorman and I had to solve. And what about the mayor? He ordered the murder of my client's sister, and he knew San Francisco's corrupt system inside out. He surely had the power to discover the identities of his hit man and his lover's sister's private dick. The lights went out again.

Sara buzzed me. "John is here to see you."

"Send him in, dearie."

Boorman entered and immediately lost his poker face—it turned a shade of frantic. "What in Hell happened to you?"

"I don't think I have to tell you, John. Brannigan is written all over my beaten and defeated face. It reminds us of what we need to talk about. "

"Brannigan and Diamond?

"Brannigan, Diamond, and the mayor," I said. "They represent a life-and-death threat to us."

"I've got an idea."

"Shoot," I said, without thinking.

"I have a special skill, and I propose we use it to eliminate Brannigan, Diamond, and Mayor Rossini. I've already started doing preliminary research on it."

Oh, no! He was back at it again—he couldn't stop thinking and acting like a hitman. I wanted no part of this—it was haunting my life. "No! I'm not going to involve myself in targeted murder."

"But it wouldn't be murder, Matt. You'd just be defending yourself against the threat they represent. You yourself said it was a matter of life and death."

"Yes, it is, and I intend to protect myself. And I want to help you defend yourself. But I refuse to resort to Brannigan- and Diamond-type behavior. While I may be a miserable person, I feel as if I'm way better than they are." And I was not prepared to once again struggle with a sniper or hitman's guilt. The war was supposedly over.

"Okay then, what can we do?"

"Play Brannigan and Diamond off against one another," I said.

"What do you mean?"

"I highly suspect that, at this point, they fear and hate each other. What would happen, then, if we somehow brought them together? Would they talk things out like diplomats? Or would they draw on each other like Wild West cowboys? I'm guessing that it might turn into a gun battle. Since this is America, let's give them the freedom and the opportunity…to kill each other."

"How could we get them together?"

"Do you have a place where you usually meet Diamond for

job assignments?"

"Yes, there's a bench in front of a field house in Gateway Park."

"Does it usually happen at night when the field house is closed?"

"Yes, exactly."

"Perfect. You'll call Diamond and give him some excuse for why you had disappeared after the Martin hit. You'll tell him that you want to talk further about it and perhaps discuss a new job. Then you'll arrange to meet him on the bench at your usual time, if you guys have one."

"Yes, then what?"

"Next, I'll call Brannigan and warn him to stop the belligerence toward me, or I'll rat him out to the press and his bosses. I'll both scare and enrage him. Then I'll propose that we meet to discuss things further at that bench, your place in Gateway Park.

"Brannigan and Diamond will show up to meet us and end up encountering and confronting each other," I hoped.

Boorman's tightened jaw and curled lips expressed doubt. "I don't know. Won't they immediately realize it's a set-up?"

"Yes, they probably will. But they won't be able to turn their backs on one another and just walk away. They can't take that risk. I suspect that each will be tempted to confront the other right there."

"Hmm, yes, maybe….it sounds better and better the more I think about it." He stood up and started walking around. Even when just planning a job, he trod lightly.

"Would Diamond bring a back-up force, fearing that you might be trying to get rid of him?"

"I don't know. Of course, he had never done anything like

that before, but I guess he could hide them in the park this time. He could see this meeting as a potentially threatening situation," said Boorman. "I don't think so, but I can't say for certain." He sat back down.

"Though Brannigan is a coward, I don't believe he'd want backup around to see him meeting me in the park. It might suggest to his partners in crime that things are falling apart for him. That wouldn't be a good look."

"How will we know what happens—big shootout or no?"

"We'll be watching everything from inside the closed and darkened field house—assuming, of course, the meeting is at nighttime," I said.

"Yes, great idea! That could work." He broke out in what looked like a broken smile, which, for Boorman, apparently meant high enthusiasm.

"We'd need to deal with the mayor differently, though. It would require a performance that would be a challenge to pull off. I would work on his ego by pretending that I was an East Coast reporter—from Philadelphia or New York—who wanted to profile his accomplishments as mayor. Toward the end of the interview, I would bring up Barbara Martin and hint that I might start spreading their relationship around in the press. The goal would be to scare him into walking away from everything—resigning in other words," I said.

"He has a reputation as being an impossible, bullheaded man. And he still holds a lot of power. I don't know if that would work, Matt."

"Well, do you have another idea? One that doesn't require you and me to pull triggers?"

"No, not at the moment."

"Then let's at least give it a try. Would you like to drink on it?"

"Yes, I could use one."

We sat around drinking Bacardi for a while, supposedly adding body and soul to the plan, but then I felt it was time to begin putting it in motion. "Can you reach Diamond now?"

"Maybe. Would we call from here?"

"Oh no, no—not Diamond's call. I don't know if he could trace it or not, but it would be a disaster if he did. C'mon, I know where we can go."

We drove to San Francisco's bus depot. It was large, noisy, and anonymous, with plenty of large phone booths curtained for privacy. We entered one.

"John, handle the call with Diamond the way you think best. Choose a meeting date that's convenient for him."

I deposited a dime into the phone, and Boorman tilted the receiver so that I could hear everything. Our call rang.

"Yeah, hello."

"I want to speak with Chance."

"Whose on the line?"

"Tell him it's John Boorman."

A few seconds later, Diamond came to the phone. "Yeah, John? Where in the world have you been?" he said urgently. "We've been worried to death about you!"

"I'll bet. I just needed to take a little break after the last job."

"Why—is there anything wrong?"

"No, not at all, Chance. I was just tired." He sounded like it.

"Are you sure there's nothing wrong?"

"No, nothing at all. But we can talk a little more about it if you want. And I'd also like you to give me another job. I need the money and something to do. Can we get together?"

"Sure, John, sure. How about if we meet at the usual place

86

and time tomorrow? Nine o'clock in the pm?"

"I'll be there."

"Goodbye, John."

We hung up the phone. "He's never signed off so abruptly," said Boorman. "Diamond avoided his usual small talk."

"Maybe he's never been so disappointed with you before," I said. "He may think it calls for a permanent solution."

We returned to my office and prepared the other half of the meeting. I was a little too excited and needed another drink to calm myself down. I finished it in a couple of gulps.

"John, what's the name of that field house?"

"DeBeau."

"Is there any chance that Brannigan knows where you guys usually meet?"

"I highly doubt it."

"Okay, here we go!" I dialed the detective bureau and tilted the receiver so that Boorman, his head next to mine, could hear everything Brannigan said. Our call rang.

"Hello, I'd like to speak with Lieutenant Brannigan."

"Who should I say is calling?"

"Matt Moulton."

"Just the minute."

It literally took a minute before Brannigan picked up the call. "Yeah, whaddya want, Moulton?"

"It's simple. I want you to leave me alone. I know you were behind my back-alley beating last night. You were afraid to try doing it yourself, and so you sent a couple of goons after me. I know a lot about you, Brannigan, and I won't hesitate to reveal it all publicly if you don't stop your cowardly belligerence."

There was silence on the other end for about ten seconds. "I take it this is a blackmail call?"

"No, not at all—I don't give a shit about money. I just want to get together with you and hash this thing out so that I can work in peace again. By the way, if anything happens to me, everything about you will automatically come spilling out. And remember: That includes some luridly juicy stuff."

There was a nasty harrumph and then a pregnant silence. "Okay, when and where do you want to get together?"

I feared that he wouldn't buy my time and place—then what? It would be curtains for the plan. "Uh, let's see…how about tomorrow night at nine in Gateway Park? There's a bench in front of the LaBeau Field House that would be an ideal place to meet."

Again, Brannigan took a long while to respond. He loathed not having the advantage, not being in charge. "Why that part of the park?"

"Because it's quiet and deserted there. I don't think you want to meet in a crowd. But I'm warning you now: If you don't show up at nine, I'll just leave."

"Okay, I'll be there, Moulton."

"And don't forget, Lieutenant, don't bring your stiffs along with you."

It sounded as if he slammed the phone down. Good. I was hoping he felt frightened and frustrated at the same time.

I wiped my brow—this time, I really was sweating. But I felt good.

"Where do you think this leaves us?" asked Boorman.

"I tend to be cynical and pessimistic. But this time, I feel we're sitting in the catbird seat." Now, if only we could stay up there. I was more than happy to arrange the meeting where Brannigan and Diamond could settle their differences. Forever and ever.

Chapter Twelve

The sprawling Gateway Park was a beautiful, bustling place—in the daylight. It beckoned people with its rich greens, blues, browns, grays, and yellows, a mix of mini-forests, ponds, baseball diamonds, painted picnic areas, and majestic field houses, all sitting under California's golden sun. People could be their best selves in Gateway Park—in the daylight.

At night, all that could change. The dark and lonely corners of the park could be hiding places for people to be their worst selves, their secret predatory selves. When I was a detective in the bureau, it was at night when we were called to investigate rapes and murders in Gateway. It was also the nighttime place where Chance Diamond would go to plot and assign his contract killings. Yes, the park was a different place in the dark, and that's where we went to stage and observe our own work—that carefully arranged, potentially deadly meeting between Brannigan and Diamond. We were just being ourselves, and perhaps that was the best and the worst of it as well.

Around eight-thirty that night, Boorman and I examined the bench area in front of the park's LaBeau Field House. I could see firsthand why Diamond used it for his meetings. It was deep in the park, hidden by the forest on one side and on the right arm of the embracing field house on the other. It was desolate there at night—a perfect setting and situation for misbehavior and mayhem.

We let ourselves into the field house and made sure there was no security man on guard. Boorman knew his way around, directly leading me to the right arm of the building, whose large window looked out over that all-important bench just twenty-five or so feet away. We opened the window to help us see and hear the meeting, but we had to be careful to stay out of the window's smudged-over sightlines. Getting caught could mean our lives. We kneeled down below the ledge.

About a minute before nine, we saw a tall, wide-shouldered man approaching from the left, walking on the darkened part of the sidewalk between the lights. I couldn't identify Brannigan's face until he fell under the light of the nearest pole over our window. He looked nervous. The lieutenant stopped at the bench but didn't sit down—he was too busy turning his head this way and that, casing the general area. He waited, his right hand holding something in his black overcoat pocket, his left hand tugging on the bill of his charcoal gray hat.

About two minutes after nine, another man came into view, not from the sidewalk on the left or right, but directly from the pathway in the black-green forest straight ahead. He ultimately reached the edge of the light, revealing a short, stubby, hatless, tieless figure with a head full of oily, graying black curls and a pockmarked face with a wise-guy expression. He was Chance Diamond, and he was the first one to speak.

"Lieutenant? Lieutenant Brannigan? What the Hell are you doing here?'

"I was going to ask you the same question, Diamond. Is this a set-up?"

"A set-up? What the fuck are you talking about?"

Diamond looked cool, but Brannigan seemed more nervous than ever. "We weren't scheduled to meet each other here," said the Lieutenant in a suppressed tone of voice.

"No, we weren't. But as long as we're here, I want to talk to you about something." He looked at his watch and then turned left and right to see if anyone was coming. "Please sit down a quick minute."

Brannigan reluctantly sat down, but he left a lot of space on the bench between himself and Diamond. He looked around. His right hand remained in his pocket.

"Lieutenant, somebody in your office has been talking to the press about Barbara Martin. Stories appeared in the Chronicle on consecutive days. What's going on there?"

"I don't know. Nobody on my team has said anything to the papers."

"Then how did the stories get written? Did the reporter make up the articles? Was he psychic?" Diamond narrowed his eyes and smirked. "Somebody must have told him something. Need I remind you that I'm paying you good money to keep this case as quiet and undercover as the deepest grave?"

Though it was hard to notice, Brannigan inched away. "We always keep our mouths shut. We don't have any stoolies."

Diamond had been talking in a smooth and subdued manner. But now his voice was getting a little more vehement and agitated. "Then why are all these details coming out, such as that business about Martin having a child and Martin being someone called Worthington? What's going to come out next—the fact that she was the mayor's girlfriend? Your people have to shut their mouths."

Brannigan raised his voice above his earlier mumble but

didn't sound any more convincing. "I'm telling you that we're not the snitchers, Diamond. The information is coming from somewhere else."

Diamond bent his face forward. "From where? Who else knows all that stuff? Lieutenant, I'm not going to jail because you can't do your job protecting us. You're taking our money without working for it. In fact, you're being sloppy. This must stop. Now."

Impulse took over: Brannigan stood up and pulled out his gun. He didn't shoot—he just stood there, pointing the revolver at Diamond. Brannigan seemed surprised at himself: He was accustomed to others doing the dirty work for him. But Diamond showed no such hesitation. He rapidly removed a large gun from underneath his jacket and blew a hole through Brannigan's chest. The lieutenant reeled, and his gunned hand wilted. Then, to finish him off, Diamond put the gun close to the lieutenant's face and took a shot that obliterated it to Hell. You were apparently not going to draw on Diamond and get away with it. He checked his nauseating work and started to walk away.

It was then that everything spiraled out of my control. Or better yet, it was then that the illusion of my control died a violent death. Boorman stood up and shot twice through the open window. The bullets hit Diamond's back and knocked him over. At first, I couldn't give voice to my feelings—I didn't know what they were exactly. Finally, I said, "John, why the fuck did you do that?"

"Because it didn't go as we planned. They were supposed to eliminate each other, but that didn't happen. I wasn't going to let Diamond walk away and continue planning my murder. I know him: He'd find me no matter where I'd go. And he might discover your identity as well. Once that happened, you wouldn't be around for too much longer, either. Now we got what we came for—they died together."

"But now you've made me an accessory to murder," I futilely said. "A hit man-style murder."

"I'm sorry, Matt. I really appreciate all you've done for me. But I must be concerned about my own survival. I couldn't allow Diamond to live. It was an act of self-defense," he said in a cold, hard voice.

I was no goody two shoes. I saw that we were both right: I recognized his truth, but it didn't make mine any easier to live with.

After a short wait to see if backup arrived, we walked outside and looked over the dead. Boorman wiped his gun with a handkerchief and put it in Brannigan's hand. He took Brannigan's gun, looked it over, and put it in his own pocket. It wasn't even a police gun that could be traced to him. Brannigan apparently planned to shoot me with it, leave it behind, and then take off. "We better get out of here," Boorman said.

As we drove back to the office, I thought about fate and inevitability. Was it fate that made Amy Worthington choose me as her dick—and did that make it inevitable that I would end up here, an accessory to murder? Why in the world did I become a gumshoe, venturing in and out of the moral darkness? What was the ultimate cause of my current plight? Was it my long-ago agreement to kill people as a wartime sniper and assassin? I couldn't seem to escape that part of my life. My past haunted my present and just shot a hole into my future.

We sat down in the office and had a couple of whiskeys. I also needed to light a cigarette. The smoke hovered over my head like the unwanted past. "John, I got you a job in Paris working for Pierre LaCroix, an associate of mine from the war years. He was part of the French underground. He runs a legitimate business, and so if you're going to work for him, you can't be killing people on the side. No more Diamonds. LaCroix gave up his sniping in Vichy during the war."

"Don't worry, I won't be doing that. The murder business ends here in San Francisco."

"Sara will give you his address and phone number and provide you with a fake passport and visa. But she'll need your photograph."

"Okay, I'll get her one. Now, what are you going to do regarding the mayor?"

"I interview him tomorrow. I'll let you know how it turns out." As a dick, I've often had to pretend to be someone else. To put myself in the mood to be the news reporter tomorrow, I planned to wear phony, brown-rimmed glasses. I was hoping that they would make me look and feel like a wordsmith. That was probably impossible.

"But I'm also concerned about the police chief's role in all of this. If he's involved, we have to worry about him."

"Matt, as a private detective, you know that this is a nasty system, full of corruption. That's why it proved so lucrative for Diamond and Brannigan. We want to survive this situation, but we have to realize that we can't solve every potential problem, can't avoid every possible danger."

Boorman was being coldly realistic—he was rightfully concerned only with self-survival. In my case, survival involved two people—both Gina and myself.

But I had another obligation: I always dedicated myself to the cause of my clients, no matter how sleazy, selfish, dirty, or disreputable they might be. You wouldn't be a very good gumshoe or a very popular one if you didn't always do what was best for the people who hired you. While I never played the avenging angel, I owed it to Amy, Dorothy, and her child to make life as hard as possible for the mayor.

But I didn't intend to be judge, jury, and executioner. There was only so far I was willing to go. I was a dick and nothing more.

Chapter Thirteen

I had an appointment with a cold-blooded killer. He wasn't part of the mob. He wasn't a convicted felon. Rather, he was the elected mayor of San Francisco, maybe one of the most corrupt cities in California. Through his press secretary, the mayor jumped at the chance to interview with me. It would enable him to talk about his favorite voter—himself. And he no doubt hoped that the prestige of a news story from a supposed East Coast reporter could help him retain power—including the power to order murders—for a while longer.

Even after a lot of prep, I felt tense when I arrived at the municipal offices with my pad and pen. I feared that the press secretary, a bald guy with a small gray beard and an officious manner, would ask me for identification. I hoped that he would be too busy and distracted for that.

The bill of my fedora was turned up in what I perceived to be the best reporter's style. The glasses completed my guise, though they magnified my eyes and blurred my vision a little more than I appreciated. "Hi, pal. I'm scheduled to interview the mayor. My name is Clark Roulston." I said.

He recoiled as he studied my battle-ravaged face. I recoiled as I took in his cheesy, spot-marked, brown-checkered suit. We were already at odds. "Oh, ah, yes, Mr. Roulston, you're with The Philadelphia Inquirer, aren't you? May I see your credentials?"

"Oh, sure." I pulled out my wallet and made a showy attempt to find credentials that weren't there. "Well, can you beat that—I guess I left my press ID in the hotel room. But I can go back and get it. It would take me only an hour or so."

"That won't be necessary, Mr. Roulston. His honor is unusually busy today and can't sit around waiting. You may go right in." He gave me a relaxed frown, which I gathered was his version of a smile. I was relieved that he was in no mood to challenge me—or, more likely, my face.

I entered a cavernous office with too much municipal furniture, much of it more than twenty years old. A heavy metal desk sat at the center of the room, and standing behind its chair and looking out the window in an artificial pose was a rather tall, husky man in a too-tight olive suit. He theatrically turned around.

"Mr. Roulston, how do you do?" He had a good-looking, dark, square face, but his Mediterranean features were informed by impatience and the slightest suggestion of irritability. Wasn't it a burden when the voters expected you to work for your power?

"I'm pleased to meet you, Mayor Rossini."

"Please take a seat, Mr. Roulston. Now, what brings you to my office all the way from Philadelphia?" he said with a two-bit smile. Rossini stared at my face but was too diplomatic to say anything. He sat down in a chair that creaked.

"I've been writing a series of articles profiling the most effective mayors across the country. My editor believes they'll inform our readers about what works at this level of government. Given your accomplishments, you were next in line for an article." In truth, I suspected that he had no accomplishments at all—at least no accomplishments that benefited anyone but himself.

He brightened, but the look of impatience never left his face. If I were guessing, I would say that, in addition to taking on the required government and political responsibilities, this was a guy who had his hands in many tills and many pockets, and the stress of managing everything could sometimes become too much for him. "Well, I'd be happy to answer any questions about my, er, our success."

I wanted him to relax and become complacent before I put him on the spot regarding Martin/Worthington. I asked him a series of questions he could drone on about. He talked about the economy, upcoming cultural projects, street maintenance, education, police, fire, and crime. I now had my opportunity to go after him.

"Mayor, getting back to crime, what do you know about the recent Barbara Martin murder?"

He winced. It was as if my sentence slapped him in the face. He realized that his expression gave something away, and so he made a too-obvious effort to mask the feeling with a verbal distraction—a way of slightly rephrasing things. "Barbara Martin, you say. Hmm, no, I don't believe I've heard of that case." His chair creaked again, more loudly this time.

"Yes, mayor, Barbara Martin. She was murdered in a downtown office building a couple of weeks ago. What was tragic about it was that her little daughter witnessed the murder. That would be a hard case to forget."

He stared hard at the surface of his desk. "Oh, that's really sad," he said with wide eyes and no emotion. This guy was as cold as a tombstone in a Chicago winter. "No, I'm not familiar with a Barbara Martin and her daughter."

"Martin headed a company called Worth Import/Export."

"I don't believe I've ever heard of that business."

"I understand it was one of your city's thriving enterprises."

"I can't know about every one of them." The mayor was looking everywhere but at me.

"Well, now, mayor, you can be honest with me. I happen to know that you had been dating a woman by the name of Barbara Martin for the last few years. And I understand you two had a child together. It was a pretty cozy affair." I softened the blow with a toothy, all-American smile.

He finally shot me a look. "I beg your pardon, Mr. Roulston. You're making unsubstantiated accusations. I am a happily married man."

"I can support what I say. I even have pictures. But, Mayor, dating a woman who's not your wife and fathering a child with her are not your biggest problems. Don't forget there's a murder involved here."

His expression was loaded—the bugged eyes and grimacing lips were ready to finish me off right now. "How dare you? Are you actually accusing me of murder?" His voice got louder than I believe he intended. After all, he didn't want to share our discussion with potential gossipers in the office, including a pressman who may have had his ear at the door this very moment.

I smiled and waved a hand. "Oh, no, no—don't get me wrong mayor. I'm not accusing you of pulling any trigger," I said softly, trying to calm things down.

The fire in his eyes disappeared—for a couple of seconds.

"But I do have proof that you arranged Barbara Martin's murder. I promise you, though, that I won't make that public provided you agree to step down from office. Voters wouldn't be happy knowing that their mayor took out a contract on somebody. It wouldn't be right to sicken or frighten them with that knowledge. I mean, what would San Francisco parents tell their poor children?"

He stood up. "Mr. Roulston, where did you get the temerity to walk in here and make those charges? You don't seem to know who I am and the power I wield."

"Yes, I know who you are: You're a corrupt mayor who murdered someone who became inconvenient for you. And now you're in danger of the public finding out."

He stabbed at the air in the direction of the door. "Roulston, get out of my office!"

The mayor clicked on his intercom: "Leo, call security—I'm being threatened."

That sounded like my cue to get out of there, especially if I wanted to dodge another beating—or worse. I slipped out of the two offices, skidded on the freshly mopped lobby floor, and—barely keeping my balance—virtually slid into the elevator going down. A large man from the mayor's office ran toward me. He reached out for the elevator door, but it just closed on him. I avoided his clutches by a fingertip.

I left the building, but—because it was still morning—the foot and car traffic was so light that the security man might have been able to spot me on the street. So I ducked into an alley and hid behind some garbage cans. My angry-faced pursuer surprised me by choosing the alley for his search and then nicely offering his back to me. Taking advantage of the split seconds I had to work with, I grabbed him around the neck, thrust my knee into his spine, and jerked his body violently backwards. He wailed so loud that I feared it would attract police or other passersby. As he lay on his back, I kicked him in the side for good measure—"give my best to your boss," I said. I then casually left and strolled over to my car, whistling along the way. I was happy to escape: The city hall alley's rancid rat and refuse odor alone almost killed me, or at least my sense of smell. And where would a dick be without his nose?

As I drove, I knew my way home, but I felt as if I wasn't going to get there. Reality became a roadblock. I suddenly felt lost—I was physically drained and mentally sidetracked. The Worthington/Martin/Boorman case turned pitch black, and I could no longer see my way through it. I wasn't sure if I could muster the energy to even try. Five people died, a child lost her mother, and I suffered two beatings, one almost fatal. With its revelation of the city's assassination business, the case revived harrowing memories of my own nasty past. Yet, the person most responsible for setting this mess in motion would apparently walk away with his reputation and power intact. My plan for the corrupt mayor's future was a total failure, like everything else about this case. Yes, I found myself lost in a place called nowhere.

Now, because of that failure, Gina and I were perhaps more vulnerable than ever to the police and their governing bosses. That was why I was seriously considering the possibility of leaving San Francisco and moving my dick operations south to the so-called city of angels. The people there would be morally dark, too, and that was good news for a private snoop. I also hoped it would be less officially corrupt, making it easier and less dangerous for a gumshoe to ply his daily trade. But was that realistic? I was probably engaging in wishful thinking about LA as well as failing to consider that SF's bad guys would follow me there or wherever I fled. There was nowhere to hide.

I imagined I would be able to recruit Sara and her family to come along with me, especially if I gave them financial help to move. But what could I do about Gina? Could I ask her to move south without committing myself to marriage? If I loved her, shouldn't I marry her?

I returned to the office, downed two short drinks, and made two calls. I called Gina first, arranging to meet her after work at the Blue Drop Inn, our favorite lounge. Then I called Boorman with the bad news about our city leader.

"John, the ploy didn't work. I seemed to anger the mayor more than scare him. He sent a security brute after me, but thankfully, the guy was dumber than average. I took care of him in the alley. But no, I didn't kill him," I said with a raised voice.

"Of course, you didn't," he said as he tested out a laugh. "But Matt, I didn't think the mayor was going to succumb to pressure either. Now, he may soon find out who you are and where you work and live. You have to be especially careful."

"I may leave San Francisco altogether—possibly for Southern California."

"Rossini has a long reach. You'll have to be looking over your shoulder there as well."

"Yeah, I thought about that, John. But I'm very accustomed to looking over my shoulder—after all, I wouldn't want my past to catch up with me. When are you leaving for Paris?"

"Oh, not for a few days yet. I still have some things to do."

"Good luck to you there. Please stay out of trouble—you know, like I'm doing."

He seemed to chuckle again. "Thanks for everything, Matt! So long."

I assumed that with Boorman gone, everything would get

at least a little better—the fog might not dissipate, light might not fill the darkness, rainbows might not appear, but life would improve. The lifelong cynic in me was suddenly being very unrealistic again and—indeed—almost compromising my dick attitude.

Chapter Fourteen

The Blue Drop Inn was a large, smoky, music-filled lounge that was so loud it was intimate and private: You could talk about anything without anyone overhearing or interrupting. It gave a small stage to jazz-swing acts, but that was only on weekends. During the week, a large jukebox, with the best selection of pop and jazz-swing anywhere, played almost continuously. The jukebox alone must have made management rich.

When we entered, almost everyone seemed to recognize us. It was no wonder: We used to spend many hours with the regulars in this place—it was like home for us and maybe even more important than home for many of them. If time dissipated their specific memories of me, they certainly couldn't forget us as a couple, the hard-looking white guy in the hep fedora and the black beauty in hot, jazzy, glad rags. And she didn't disappoint anyone tonight, dressed in her shapely and snug black jacket with white buttons, slim white skirt, and flat white hat with black stripes. Some people were clothes horses. Gina was a clothes pony—a prize one.

We squeezed into a tiny booth, quickly ordered drinks, and proceeded to crack wise and cute. This was one time when the music was working against us: The jukebox was playing the sweetly melancholic "Stormy Weather" by the great Lena Horne, and the song seemed more appropriate for my dick life than my love life. But then again, maybe it was trying to tell me something about our love life.

I advised Gina that her beauty was making her look bad. "Everybody wonders why someone like you can't find a better-looking boyfriend," I said. She laughed and said "Pretty boys don't interest me. I like my guys rough around the edges." I laughed without mirth.

"Really though, I've had all kinds of boyfriends. You're not even my first white guy."

"Honestly?" I couldn't read her because her eyes suddenly became aloof.

"I attended a mixed-race high school in Oakland, and my first crush in freshman year was a white boy. Every day, I'd smile at him, and he'd smile at me, and we'd talk to each other a little, but we were both too shy to go beyond that. Besides, there was that border—that black/white line that we dared not cross. You think it's hard now for us as an adult couple, but can you imagine dating someone of another race in high school—before the war? The other kids, mainly the white ones, would never have accepted it." She dragged thoughtfully on her cigarette.

"Well, I'm glad nothing ever happened. If it had, I'd be in love right now with a married woman, the mother of two coffee- and crème-colored kids. What could I have done about that?" Gina smiled, this time with both her eyes and her mouth.

When we tired of the clever back-and-forth, I turned the talk over to more immediately important matters.

"Precious, what happened when people in the office heard about Brannigan's death?"

"There was shock, but—honestly speaking—I didn't detect too much sympathy. A couple of his closest henchmen grieved, but that was as far as it went."

"Was there any talk about the Martin case? Or about the dear departed's connection to the gang lord who killed him?"

"There was a lot of whispering and shifty-eyed talk, but too much of it took place in deserted corners and behind closed doors."

"Any suspicion directed at you?"

"Nobody there takes me seriously unless they need something done. If anyone was suspicious of me, it was Brannigan, and now he's gone." Gina surprised me by crossing herself.

"His cronies might know about his suspicions," I said.

"I haven't noticed anything like that so far."

"Do you know who's taking over for Brannigan?"

"No, I heard no announcement yet."

"That's the next guy we'll need to worry about—the guy who takes Brannigan's job and inherits his dirty contacts. This is a case that never ends—and keeps getting darker and darker. I feel like I'm drowning in a cesspool, all but submerged by corrupt cops, paid hit men, lying clients, and a murderous mayor. The case has brought back my worst nightmares from the war…"

"You mean about your time as a sniper in France?" asked Gina.

"Yes, and it's driving me away—I'm thinking about moving my gumshoe business south."

"You would leave San Francisco?" She seemed surprised and almost hurt. "How would that allow you to escape the war?"

She came to the point with a great question, and the real answer was that there was no escape from the past war in

106

France or from the current war in San Francisco. So, I just ignored the question. "I asked you out tonight because I wanted to know if you'd leave with me."

"Leave with you? What does that mean, Matt? Are you asking me to marry you?" She widened her eyes and mashed out her cigarette. Gina was making things difficult—why couldn't I ask her that question without having to make a commitment? Why was tying yourself to marriage such an obsession with everyone, especially women?

"I wasn't thinking about marriage right away, but yes, we'd eventually do that. You know I love you."

She was thoughtful for a long time. She sipped her drink and took out another cigarette. "Matt, I love you. I don't think I could ever love anyone more than I love you."

"I hate to hear you say that because it sounds as if a big 'but' is coming."

"Do you remember when I said that race was the reason you ended our relationship the first time?"

"Yeah, of course."

"That wasn't fair of me. If you did end it for that reason, you were probably right to do so." She raised her brows and lowered her face.

"Why would you say that now?"

"Because, as I've told you, I've been thinking and understanding a lot more over the last few months. The truth is that people won't let us love each other." She waved her lit cigarette around and smiled sadly. "Oh, in places like this, where everyone's drinking and dancing all the time, they'll see us and say, 'Oh, how amusingly daring,' and they'll look the other way for a few hours. But everywhere else, many or most people will treat us as if we're breaking a law or violating a moral code. In the end,

I think they're just following the everyday racism that they feel so comfy with the prejudice they learned growing up. It's part of the American way."

"So why do we have to accept that? Why do we care what other people think?"

"Matt, your first reaction is to fight everything and everyone. How will you fight this? One day, you'll be fighting a turned-back, a cross look, or a nasty comment. Another day you'll be fighting outright discrimination—the client who won't hire you or the cop who won't give you a break because your wife is a Negro. And what about me? What about our children? Do you want us to fight every day, too? Is that fair? How do we do that? What power do we have? How do we become a black-and-white family in a white-dominated society?"

"But sweetheart so much has changed since the war," I said gamely. "I mean, it's 1949, it's the future!"

"And in your very limited experience with dating a Negro, what exactly has changed since the war? Haven't you com-plained, over and over again, about how difficult people have made it for us because we were a mixed couple?"

I loved to contend with her. But I couldn't argue with her now because she was right about everything, and that broke my heart. It broke into little pieces with a hammer. She was essentially saying that we couldn't be together because it represented a naked challenge to a society that had a knock against Negroes. If America didn't try to exclude them, there would be nothing unusual about a black-and-white couple. Instead, Gina and I would stand out as a symbol against the way things were, and it would antagonize people by reminding them of their intolerance and prejudices.

She looked apprehensive. "Matt, you're not saying anything."

"You've left me speechless, dear. I can't dispute anything you've said. But please hold off—don't make any rash and final decisions. The world can still change, and we can change along with it."

"You're going to put off marriage just to wait for me?" Her eyes begged for an answer.

"Well, you know I'm not exactly the marrying type anyway. If I can't marry you, I'm not going to run out and look for someone else to share an address with. But you—you might want to find a husband, and that possibility makes me feel sad."

"I don't feel the urgency to marry right now. And what can I do—I still love you."

"But wouldn't the security of marrying somebody be appealing to you right now?"

"No, I wouldn't be interested unless he was a certain white private eye." She didn't break into a grin until after the statement sat in the air for a few seconds.

"But I'm worried about your being in San Francisco alone. What happens if the mayor and your employer—the police— find out what you know about their corrupt connections?"

"Matt, I'm a big girl—I can take care of myself. At the very least, I must desperately try. You can't spend your life worrying about me, especially if we end up living apart." She bit into her glass of bourbon and looked straight past me—somewhere I couldn't see.

As Gina delivered that sad news, I tried to figure why we were drifting apart despite our feelings for one another. Yes, of course, race sabotaged things. But it seemed that our relationship also became another casualty of this case. It was the case where everybody and everything went to die.

109

Chapter Fifteen

I was a couple days away from leaving San Francisco for good. Sara and I were packing up the office for the final move to Southern California. With my financial help, she and her family would be joining me there as I sought to establish my dickdom in a new land. With everything well underway, I left the office for another evening date with Gina at the Tenderloin. It was our "goodbye for now" rendezvous, a sad and sweet affair of watching each other bleed to the rhythms of jazzy, bluesy swing. At one point, the band played the most downbeat and brooding version of "On the Sunny Side of the Street" we had ever heard. But for us, the song was optimistic—we would have welcomed even just a lighter form of shade in our lives.

We finally left the Tenderloin at about 1:00 am, walking a couple blocks through the fog to my car. I went to unlock the passenger door to let Gina in, and the next and last feeling I had was of the world crashing down on my head. Everything went black. It was as sudden as death. I was gone.

Minutes, hours, days, weeks, months, or years later—it was hard to tell—I woke up in a state of cloudy, thundering pain. I would have done anything for the two aspirin that we had given Boorman when he returned to consciousness. But an agonizing headache was the least of my problems. My arms and legs were tightly bound to a heavy wooden chair. Even worse, poor Gina was tied to another chair ten feet away, and some kind of dirty, oil-stained rag was stuffed into her mouth. We sat amid rows and stacks of large boxes in what looked to be some kind of warehouse with dull, buzzing lights. I would have been surprised to learn that the temperature in the place was as warm as 40 degrees.

"Well, lookie here, Matt Moulton has awakened. Isn't that sweet?" said the first man with a gun. He was a sliver of a thug with jet-black hair, dilated eyes, and an abundance of nerves. He was dynamite waiting for the spark.

The second guy with a gun was a placid and plodding type, someone older, larger, heavier, and more amorphous. I'd bet that it was his indefinite mass that had come down on my head. The clod's attack probably ruined my hat. "Your colored girlfriend has been lonely without you, pal," he gibed.

The future looked bleak for Gina and me. At this point, my only question was, "How do we put off the worst for as long as possible?" There was seemingly no way out. They had removed the gun from my breast holster. The derringer might still be under my pant cuff, but—with bound hands—there was no way to reach it.

"Hey, what's wrong with you dopey shitheads?" I asked.

"Uh, oh. It sounds like you want trouble, Moulton," said grinning gunman two.

"No, I want to know why you're being unnecessarily cruel? Why have you stuffed a rag down Gina's throat? She's not going to scream. And even if she did, nobody could hear her in this place."

The two men looked at each other and almost shrugged their

shoulders. The bigger man then shuffled over and removed the rag from Gina's mouth.

"Now, how about loosening our ropes?"

"Right. What are you going to ask for next, champagne and caviar?" said gunman one, with a dismissive laugh.

"What are you scared of? You guys have all the hardware. Isn't that enough of an advantage for you? You need more? You also want me tied up to make absolutely sure that I don't get the best of you? You guys are weak and timid, aren't you? Maybe a little yellow? Perhaps we can get you some police protection? Give them a call. Ask for Brannigan, and then tell him I sent you," I said with a delighted air.

"You know, if it was up to me, I'd kill you right now, smartass. But you better be careful, I might give in to my worst instincts," said gunman one. "Don't you want to live for a little while longer? It will give you more time to eye your cute little jungle bunny." He raised his eyebrows and snickered.

"Give me your gun and go remove their ropes," said gunman two to gunman one. It was his masculine vanity at work—he didn't want anyone thinking he was yellow.

The underling rolled his eyes and reluctantly followed orders. I felt relieved to be relatively free again. So apparently did Gina—she flashed me a tired smile.

Gunman two handed gunman one his pistol back. Now, three of us were armed: With my blood circulating again, I could feel the derringer under my pant cuff.

It sounded as if someone just entered the huge room and was clip-clopping down the concrete floors toward our area. That person ultimately materialized out of the main row: It was an oily, graying, overdressed man with shiny, expensive shoes—in other words, a city politician. It was our distinguished mayor.

"Mr. Moulton, nice to see you again! But that's strange: You don't seem like much of a wise guy today. Where's your gall? What happened?"

"I don't know, Mayor, I guess it's something I eat. Your wife cooked it for me after we screwed. She said I was better in bed than you are. It was something about my having a greater reach. Gee, what was she trying to say, mayor?"

His coldly amused expression didn't change. Feeling in total control of the situation, he calmly said, "you're not funny, Moulton, you're just repulsive. Do you plan on threatening me again tonight?"

Before I could answer, the mayor pointed to gunman two and asked, "Why isn't Moulton tied up?"

The question embarrassed and stupefied the guy. He acted as if he had just been asked why his zipper was open and why he forgot to put on underwear today. After several long seconds, he finally grunted out, "Oh ah, no worries, Mr. Mayor. We completely disarmed Moulton. He won't cause us any trouble."

His head moving side to side indicated the mayor was dubious.

But I quickly changed the subject. "By the way, Mayor, I'd be happy to cause you trouble. Everything I said during our interview still goes. I will expose you as a murderer unless you resign. And if you kill me, someone else is empowered to release that information. I will guarantee it."

"Isn't that someone else your negro there?" he said with a smug smile.

"You refer to her in a nasty, disparaging tone. But, Mayor, the truth is that I wouldn't even allow you to drink Gina's bathwater—you're not good enough. Hell, I'm not good enough. And no mayor, she is NOT that someone else. She's not involved in this matter at all."

"Well then, who might that person be? What is that information, and where are you keeping it?"

"You won't find out until it's too late."

"Perhaps I could find out now by torturing you, Mr. Moulton. I get the impression that you're not as tough as you try to act," he said, with his pale little hands on his hips.

I didn't offer a clever, antagonistic response to that. I felt I was resistant to a reasonable amount of torture, but I didn't trust this guy to be reasonable—after all, he had cold-bloodedly murdered his own little girl's mother. And what if he tried to torture Gina? How long could I keep my mouth shut under that condition?

The mayor pointed to gunman one, Mister Frantic. "Hey Joe, Mr. Moulton wants a feel of the torture we had planned for him. Would you please accommodate him? Let's put on a real show for him."

Joe smirked—this was what he was waiting for and dreaming about. He eagerly stepped forward, like a child readying to claim his Christmas present. But a gun went off, and a bullet hole emerged in his neck, releasing a steady squirt of blood. He collapsed on the concrete floor. That caught the worried attention of gunman two, and so I quickly reached for my cuff, grabbed my derringer, and shot a bullseye into his brain. No blood flow there: He just toppled over before I even got the chance to learn his name. The world was a tragic place.

A man with a gun ran out of the stacks, and it was John Boorman, the apparent shooter of gunman one. His appearance shocked me, but what he did next almost literally took my breath away. He grabbed the confused and panicked mayor by the collar, shook him several times, and shot him twice in the face, right in the eyes. Gina screamed. He then tossed his bloody honor to the side as if he were throwing out the trash. The guy was ruthless despite some of his gentler, more humane instincts. Assassination became him.

For a few seconds, I couldn't form words in my mouth—I didn't have enough air. Finally, I said, "John…another hit? Couldn't we have just turned him in?"

He just stood there looking at me, his mouth shut and his manner hyper-subdued and matter-of-fact. Only his eyes seemed charged, less from what he had just done than from what he had to do now: Explain his actions to a certain naïve, child-like private dick. How does this guy survive in this world? He appeared to wonder. Of course, I sometimes wondered that, too.

"Matt. I couldn't let this guy live—he represented a threat to me and, though you may not admit it right now, a threat to you and Gina as well. The law would never have sent him to the chair or even to jail. I know you detest this kind of action, but I feel like I saved the three of us and achieved a rough justice for your client's sister and her child."

"What exactly happened? How did you get here, John?"

"When your pressure tactic against the mayor failed, I made up my mind to kill him. I leaned toward the quiet method, poisoning him and making it look like a heart attack. But in planning for it, I learned that he went to Brannigan's detectives and found out that you were the one who leaked the Martin/Worthington coverup to the press. The mayor concluded that you were the supposed journalist blackmailing him, and so he called Diamond's crew and arranged your kidnapping, torture, and ultimate assassination," he said it all with the energy and emotion of someone slicing an apple.

"As they set you up, I set them up: I would get the mayor and his two assassins in one place at one time, where and when I could eliminate them. You helped, of course, and that I wasn't expecting. I didn't know you packed an arm on your leg." He couldn't even crack a smile at his own cleverness.

"How did you know the torture and hit were going to be here?"

"I learned all that through a friendly contact on Diamond's crew. I found out everything they were going to do. After they kidnapped you and Gina, I took your car. I drove it here—it's waiting for us outside," he said. I realized again that it was intelligence—the information he gets and the way he thinks and prepares—that makes Boorman so dangerously good. He'd make a great private dick.

"John, despite my natural cynicism about everything, I'm almost—almost—startled that official mortal corruption so easily survived Brannigan and Diamond's mutual exit. The mayor, the cops, and the gang boys continue to get together and plan murder," I said, shaking my head.

"Sure, it's a continuing enterprise. And that's why we all must leave here. Matt, you can't keep being a dick in San Francisco. And Gina, you can't keep working for the police. The system is criminal, and it knows that you two outsiders know the details of how it works. It's much too dangerous to stay. Matt, I hope you're not mad at me." Despite his words, his sudden snappiness said take it or leave it.

"How could I be mad at you? You saved Gina. You saved me." We owed our lives to a hitman, who was now preaching to us about the dangers of the "system."

"Well, you can't argue with life, Matt. C'mon, let's go before the police get here."

116

As I walked to the car with my arm around Gina's waist, I started shining another light on the ledger's debits. The Martin/Worthington case now killed eight people, with a ninth—the Worthington brother—surely on the way. Now, it could still kill Gina and me. The hypocritical Boorman should have added that you couldn't argue with death, either. Hell, if a paid killer didn't know that, who would?

"How in the world did we survive tonight?" asked Gina. This usual cocksure dick was in no mood to answer her.

Chapter Sixteen

The office was now empty, but my mind was still full—in fact, it was overloaded. I was still trying to sort through the Martin/Worthington mess, pack away my wartime guilt, and come to terms with my forced move from San Francisco, possibly without my darling Gina. But I wasn't the only one with a mind. As she accompanied me around the office, looking for anything we may have inadvertently left behind, Sara was apparently also deep in thought, and she finally confronted me with some of it late in the dimming afternoon. It provided a beginning for the end.

"Matt, could we have a little talk?" she asked, with a far-away look in her eyes.

"Sure, sweetheart. Let's sit down on the window ledge." The open blinds would give me one last chance to reflect on the perpetual blinking of those hypnotic Palace lights. I lit a cigarette to help me concentrate. Sara didn't want one right now—she just folded her sleeveless arms, crossed her panted legs, and unloaded her thoughts.

"Matt, you kept mentioning how concerned you were about the police chief—Bob O'Brien—and his possible part in the police/gangland corruption that you uncovered. So I did some research on him over the last couple days and discovered something very interesting and suggestive. You need to hear about it."

"Okay, Good work. I lend you my ears."

Her eyes smiled, but her clenched lips suggested an attitude more serious and challenging.

"In talking to some of our sources in law enforcement and government, I picked up a lot of conventional biographical stuff on O'Brien. I also heard a lot of people mocking him for the usual things, such as his peculiar look and manner. You know, like you used to do. What did you call him again?"

"Oh yeah, my name for him was Santa Cross. He has the same snow-white hair and rosy-red cheeks, but the rest of him is pure chimney soot, from his mean little black eyes to his dirty, pouting mouth. He's the only man I've ever encountered who seems to wear a scowl like a carefully and proudly groomed mustache or haircut. I guess he needs to show off his contempt and hatred in the neatest, most respectable light. The man is arresting…" And if that was a lie, it was the truest one I ever told.

"Matt, stuff like that is funny, fanciful, and true. But I wanted something new and revealing, something that Josh Baumberg, at the Chronicle, might be able to tell me about the chief. Josh seems to know everything about everyone."

"I know. I shudder to hear what he knows about me," I said. "I want to remain anonymous, sometimes even to myself."

Sara looked pleasantly exasperated because my so-called wit interrupted the momentum of her thought and spiel. She probably wanted me to return to my smoking, which I quickly did. "He told me that O'Brien was married before and that he had fathered a child—a son—with that wife. But they were together only a couple of years before he left them. O'Brien

119

remarried a few years later to his current wife, and they never had any children. I asked Baumberg the name of O'Brien's only child, and he said John."

She looked down and shrugged her wide shoulders. "By itself, that didn't mean much. The world has millions of Johns—probably more than it knows what to do with. But working with you has turned me into a highly suspicious person. I always ask a lot of questions. When my husband tells me he had oatmeal for breakfast, I want to know more: Why he chose it, when he made it, how he ate it, and what he's going to make for lunch. So I also asked Josh, 'What was the maiden name of O'Brien's first wife, the mother of John?' He said he'd find out for me."

"I don't get it. Why was that important?"

Her eyes lit up. "I was just being suspicious again. It didn't become more important than that until I learned the name. It was Boorman, as in John Boorman," she said, with careful articulation. "I ran a check on him. This John served in the Army, in the Pacific Theatre. That's generally consistent with what your client John Boorman told us about his wartime experience."

Sara's revelation hit me harder than Brannigan's fist, but it was a delayed reaction. "John Boorman?! You're kidding...that must be a coincidence," I said through a billow of smoke. I should have immediately known better than that. At first, I had tried to dismiss Boorman as a coincidence in the Martin case—he couldn't have pulled the trigger, I insisted to myself. Now I was doing it again here, when it seemed very possible, even likely, that the two John Boormans were one and the same.

I suddenly felt the full impact: My mind came to life and started seizing together parts of the broken picture. It was happening so fast that I didn't even have the time to remove the cigarette from my mouth. I could see even through all the smoke in my eyes. "Wait, that's an amazing possibility, Sara—let's look at it. Our client, John Boorman, had managed to land a juicy role on a highly lucrative police/gangland hit squad. How do you bag a role that requires being accepted by two such different groups—law enforcement and organized crime? He said he got the job through mobster Chance Diamond. But did it also help to have a police father who was overseeing the whole corrupt operation?

"Of course, part of me challenges that idea. How do we know for sure that the police chief ran the hit squad? Well, we don't know that—or anything else—for certain.

But another part of me comes back with more powerful questions: Could the police chief have been unaware of an assassination service whose personnel included Lieutenant Brannigan and a slew of his other city detectives? And if he did know about it, wouldn't he insist on controlling it? After all, if the operation became public, he, the chief of police, would be the first person the DA and the politicians would target for blame and legal punishment. If he controlled it, he could keep it better hidden and easily do such things as put a struggling son on the payroll."

"I knew you'd ask the right questions, Matt. I thought some of the same things," she said. Her widened eyes goaded me for more. And in case I didn't get the hint, she squeezed my hand.

"And what happens when a hit goes haywire, two key members of your assassination squad panic and start to suspect one other, and the client ordering the hit gets blackmailed? As the chief of police, do you worry about everything falling apart and becoming public?

"To save the day, do you maybe use your hit-man son to eliminate that vulnerable client, the mayor? And are you more likely to make that move if you and the mayor are at odds in some way, perhaps politically? According to scuttlebutt, you've long wanted to be the next mayor. What could be easier—and more certain—than defeating your opponent with bullets rather than ballots?" Sara closed her eyes, nodded her head, and frowned out a smile. It appeared she could easily imagine the self-interested wickedness I described.

My eyes burned, and my mind heated up. "When I brought up my suspicion and fear of the chief of police, Boorman insisted that we couldn't worry about everything. The guy who brooded about the danger of Brannigan and Diamond somehow wasn't worried about the head guy. Why? Was he trying to protect his father? And how did Boorman find out about the planned kidnapping, torture, and assassination of Gina and me? He said his contacts told him. But could his main contact have been his father?"

I was really smoking now. "And why did he bump off Diamond, his supposed mentor and father figure? He claimed it was to protect himself. But let's be realistic here: Could Diamond have ever gotten away with killing John Boorman if Boorman's real father oversaw everything? Rather than needing to save himself, John might have whacked Diamond at the behest of his dad, who wanted to clean up the messy Martin job. Hell, John might have shot Brannigan, too, if Diamond hadn't pulled the trigger first. There's no direct courtroom evidence of anything and certainly no positive proof of family kinship, but there are giant puddles of circumstantial blood lying all around. You can't step around them."

Sara rarely smoked, but now she was taking a cigarette out of my case. I lit it for her. The first long drag seemed to provide her with tremendous relief. "Matt, I always felt dubious about John, and it was hard to say exactly why. But I hesitated to share my feelings with you mainly because of his memory loss. That seemed real to me, painfully so."

"I agree. I don't think John could have faked the memory loss and recovery, particularly the attacks he suffered when I showed him a picture of Dorothy's little girl. In fact, they seemed to almost kill him, leaving him unconscious. The girl's unexpected presence during the murder really touched and pained something deep within this professional killer.

"His resulting amnesia and then disappearance threatened to sabotage not only his own livelihood but also the whole operation. Why would he have faked something like that? It was bad for business. His spark of humanity was an instinct that created too much revealing light for everybody involved, and perhaps his father made up his mind to do whatever it took to extinguish it and then eliminate the consequences. Humanity can be a scary thing in times like this for people like that."

"But Matt, in the back of my mind, there was maybe another reason why I was reluctant to raise this seemingly wild idea of John as the police chief's son. If he was simply carrying out his supposed father's wishes, why did he leave you and Gina alive?

That didn't make any sense. With your inside knowledge, the two of you represented a dire threat to the police chief and the corrupt system underneath him. You and Gina were consequences that had to be eliminated, or so one would think."

If I ever even slightly doubted why I was taking Sara south with me, she effectively reasoned that away this afternoon. She approached the world with the street IQ and the sharply cynical attitude of the best gumshoes. What would I do without her help? She sparked my vision this afternoon.

And now she raised a reasonable doubt that challenged that vision. "Yes, Sara, I was puzzled by that, too: Letting us continue to breathe couldn't have been part of the police chief's plan."

Walking back and forth and biting into my lower lip, I soon tasted blood—a figurative victory. "Ah! We must remember that O'Brien was both John's respected boss and resented father. John didn't carry his father's name. While that would have been understandable during his time as a hit man working with the city, why didn't he use his father's name earlier in life, during his Army days, for example? Could it have been that he felt like an abandoned son who hated his father for leaving? Was that why he had kept his mother's maiden name? And why was it so hard for him to say the word "father" when, during his recovery from amnesia, I asked him about his parents?" Sara smiled broadly and moved her head up and down.

"We still don't know anything for certain. But in that kidnapping/torture/murder exercise in the warehouse, John seemed to be acting like both an insider and an outsider, doing what needed to be done for his father while also pursuing his own distinct interest, which involved paying me back for rescuing him from his mental void. Gina and I are alive today because of his declaration of independence." My dicktress puffed on that idea and found it deeply satisfying as well.

"There were at least three interests involved there: John's, the mayor's, and the police chief's. John got what he wanted and ensured that the mayor did not. But now, what about the police chief and his interest? How much time do we have left before he targets us again? I'm still trying to persuade Gina that love isn't everything—her safety matters, too. And that's why she should leave San Francisco with us."

"Matt, she really does love you. I think you'd have more success using that as a pitch." She said it sternly, but her gentle-eyed look softened the impact.

"Maybe you're right." I needed something right now, and it wasn't love. I poured myself a drink, and that killed the office bottle. It was my last call in San Francisco.

The door to the outer office opened, and somebody walked in. Now what? I reached for the .38 in my shoulder holster.

"Messenger! I have a package for Matt Moulton." Sara and I walked out there to sign for the delivery. My gun spooked the pimple-faced boy, but he'd live, probably to see a clear face in the mirror one day.

Meanwhile, I felt as if I was receiving a gift—and it turned out I was. "Hey, angel, we're still getting mail." I eagerly opened the package, and a newspaper fell out and plopped open on the floor. It was the afternoon edition of the San Francisco Chronicle. The huge headline on the front page almost shocked us both: POLICE CHIEF O'BRIEN DIES, SUFFERS MASSIVE HEART ATTACK AFTER LUNCHEON. We looked at each other with our mouths open, but neither one of us said a thing. We didn't have to. We both knew what happened. It was another hit job. O'Brien was targeted with that invisible poison. John, his son, killed him, maybe not directly but through a friendly partner or what he would have called a paid "contact."

I could see it all as if I had been there: The police chief strutting into the fancy luncheon like some big deal, depositing himself at a large table with loads of flowers, chattering with other power-playing diners, eventually taking knife and fork to his elaborate plate, stuffing his fat sour face with fine food, saying something like "this tastes delicious," and proving stupidly oblivious to the possibility of being poisoned. Two hours later, he was suffering cardiac arrest, the very last arrest of his career and his life. If it had been me in his compromised position, I would have had a fucking ham and cheese—and I would have smeared the mustard myself.

I took out the package's accompanying note and read it out loud. "Forgive me, Matt, I had to carry out one last job. This one was intensely personal, a family matter." I looked at wide-eyed Sara again and then returned to reading. "Someday, we'll get together, and I'll explain it to you. I know you hate this kind of violence, but sometimes, it's the only way to achieve a rough justice. Thanks for everything, Matt. Take care. John." Sara and I had apparently got it right about everything. Almost everything.

"It's all been so wild that I'm overwhelmed. What a case, what a world!" said a weary Sara as she removed the high-rise heels she had been clumping around in all day. Her long, naked, teal-toed feet were beautiful, but too much else distracted me right now.

It began with the lingering question of why John Boorman "offed" the police chief and made him this case's ninth victim. I guessed that he was seeking to protect Gina and me. That was his unspoken purpose.

But he explicitly expressed the "rough justice" angle again, and that seemed to be his main rationale. What I wondered was: Justice for whom? For a little girl who had lost her mother days ago? Or could it also have been for a little boy who essentially lost his father many years back? John Boorman boxed, wrapped, and put a bow on this seething case with his final act of rough justice. It was a retribution that I was sure he struggled mightily to execute. After all, the wicked police chief was still his father—

even if he had been an absent one his entire childhood. That final act now seemed somehow inevitable.

But I secretly hoped John didn't think that his rough justice would erase the past. He should have known better, based on his own recent experience with memory. The past was always returning, reminding, reshaping, haunting, and—sometimes even—attacking. It never died. Part of John Boorman would always be that abandoned child who became a disgruntled hitman. And it wasn't just John who had something to learn on that score. I realized that I, too, had to find a way to live with all my selves—including those from out of the past. Part of Matt Moulton would always be that ambivalent, co-opted, cold-blooded killer for the US Army in war-torn France. It was hard to accept that person, but I had no choice. He was me.

It was all over. In the end, there was nothing—nothing more that I could do or say except, "Sara, let's get the hell out of here."

About the Author

With nothing to his name but a GED, Michael Amedeo had no choice but to begin writing. The active voice helped him earn a BA in Political Science from the University of Illinois at Chicago and an MA in International Relations from the intellectually demanding University of Chicago. He became an award-winning creative copywriter for corporations and agencies, a freelance film critic and journalist for several newspapers and magazines, and a PR and media relations writer for still more organizations. Looking for a new writer's edge, Amedeo turned to fiction and created the stylishly embittered private dick, Matt Moulton.

SOCIAL MEDIA HANDLES:
  Facebook
  Twitter

AUTHOR WEBSITE:

MichaelAmedeo.com